Best of
VIKRAM VETAL

TINY TOT PUBLICATIONS
INDIA

Best of
Vikram-Vetal

©TINY TOT PUBLICATIONS
This Edition:-2005

Retold & Edited by
Shyam Dua

Illustrated by
Rustagi. P. R.

ISBN 81-7573-612-7

Published By:
TINY TOT PUBLICATIONS
235, Jagriti Enclave,
Vikas marg,
Delhi-110092 (INDIA)
Ph.: 2216 7314, 2216 3582,
Fax:- 91-11-22143023
E-mail: tinytotpub@hotmail.com

CONTENTS

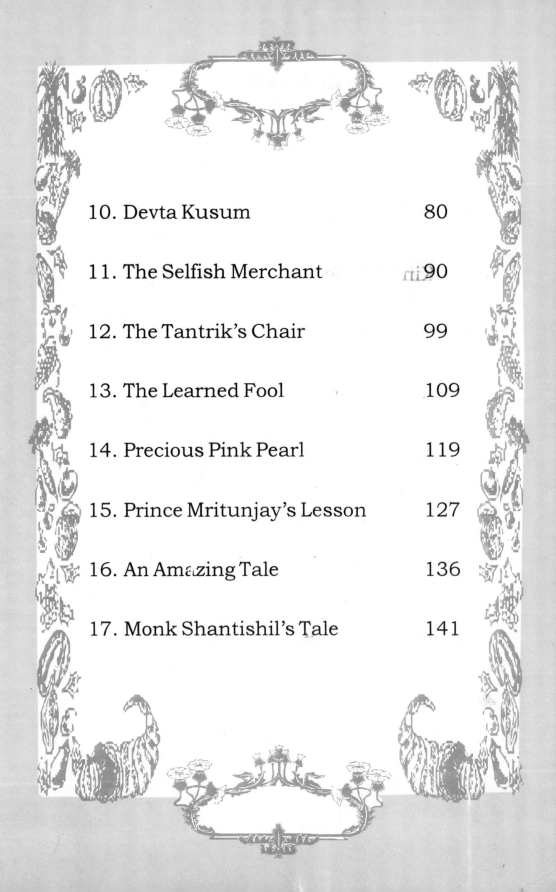

The Vikram-Vetal Tales

A long time ago, Ujjain was ruled by King Vikramaditya. He was an ideal king. He used to listen to the woes of his subjects everyday in the royal court and would do his best to help them out. The people were happy with a kind and just king ruling over them.

One day a monk came to the royal court of the King Vikram. He did not speak a word. He merely gave a custard apple (*shareefa*) to the king and left. Everyday the monk would come and offer a custard apple to the king and then leave. The king would receive the fruit and hand it over to the treasurer. One day, when the monk left after giving the fruit, King Vikram did not give the fruit to the treasurer. Instead he gave the fruit to a pet monkey of one of the royal guards. The monkey had come into the royal court and as the monkey broke the fruit into two to eat it, a large shining gem emerged out of it.

The monk had been giving one fruit each day to the king for the past ten years now, so the king asked the treasurer, "Where are the fruits we received for so many years?"

"Your Majesty," the treasurer replied, "I used to keep the fruits in the treasury. They all have spoiled now but many shining gems lie where once I had hoarded the fruits."

King Vikram grew thoughtful. The next day, when the monk arrived in the royal court, King Vikram asked, "Respected Sir, you have offered such precious gems to me for ten years now. Why have you done so?"

Then the monk spoke up for the first time. He said, "O king, I have to meditate on a certain *mantra*. For this I need the help of a brave person. I have done this to request you to help me achieve my aim."

"Yes, I promise to help you in anyway I can. What can I do for you?" said the king.

The monk said, "O king, on the *amavas* (no moon

night) a week from now I will wait for you. You must come to meet me under the banyan tree that stands in the centre of the cremation ground."

"All right, I will be there," King Vikram promised.

On the *amavas* night, King Vikram dressed himself in black clothes, put a sandalwood mark on his forehead and took up his sheathless sword in the hand. Then he left his capital city in the midnight and no one knew anything about his departure.

A few minutes later, king Vikram reached the cremation ground. It was a bit later than midnight. The only light came from some flames that still erupted from cremation fires. Skulls, skeletons and bits of bones were scattered on the whole ground of cremation. Jackals and evil spirits were producing horrifying sounds that could shake the courage of the bravest men. But King Vikram moved on fearlessly and his

naked sword was shining in the reflection of the cremation pyre flames.

Soon enough King Vikram reached the banyan tree. The monk was sitting under the tree.

King Vikram said, "Sir, I am here. Now tell me what I should do next."

"O king, you must now walk towards the Southern direction. After an hour or so you will see a big banyan tree. On a thick branch of that tree, you will find a corpse. All you have to do is to get that corpse for me to enable me to perform some rites." instructed the monk to King Vikram.

With these instructions, King Vikram left for the other banyan tree. As he was told by the monk, he soon reached the banyan tree. It had grown black due to the smoke from the cremation pyres. The foul smell of burning flesh was spreading all around the tree. On a branch, a corpse hung in a way one slings a body on one's shoulders. With great courage King Vikram approached the tree and climbed up. He took the hanging corpse from the branch and slung it on his shoulder. But the corpse slipped and fell to the ground and a loud cry of pain came out of it. It seemed as if the corpse had some life in it. As the king bent down to pick up the corpse, a laughter emmated from it. King Vikram realized that the corpse had been possessed by a Vetal. Suddenly the corpse flew up in the air and hung back on the tree branch. But brave King Vikram climbed up the tree once again and slung the corpse onto his shoulder and walked on.

After King Vikram had gone only a few steps, he heard a voice from the corpse. Vetal was speaking to King Vikram. He said, "King Vikram, you have really worked hard to climb me down. You must be very tired. To relax you and to pass our time on the tedious way ahead, I will tell you a story. But beware ! You must not speak a word while I tell the tale. If you speak up, I'll fly back to the tree where, I was hanging."

King Vikram did not reply and then the Vetal narrated an interesting tale.

King Chandrasen

King Chandrasen was a famous king who ruled over the prosperous kingdom of Ujjain. His honesty, dutifulness and love for his subjects had earned him a lot of respect. His royal court was filled with many learned scholars, philosophers and poets. He respected them a lot and they held a special place in his heart, too.

One day a scholarly priest named Shridutt from Kashi visited King Chandrasen's royal court. King Chandrasen received Shridutt with utmost respect. He offered him a grand lunch. After lunch, Shridutt, King Chandrasen and the learned scholars in the royal court, got into a discussion. They covered various subjects like justice, philosophy and religion. All the royal scholars and the king were highly impressed by the great knowledge displayed by the learned priest. After the discussion, King Chandrasen gifted a precious necklace of gems and pearls to Shridutt. Then Shridutt took his leave to go back to Kashi.

It so happened that Shridutt had to pass through a dense forest on his way from Ujjain to Kashi. As he was walking through the forest, a dacoit saw Shridutt. The necklace of gems and pearls shone bright around Shridutt's neck. At once, the dacoit desired to get the precious necklace for himself. So he took out his sharp knife and confronted Shridutt. After a few minutes' struggle, Shridutt was stabbed to death by the dacoit and the dacoit took the beautiful necklace.

By chance, some of King Chandrasen's spies were roaming around the forest. They saw the dacoit stabbing Shridutt. They rushed and caught the dacoit red handed. Then the dacoit was produced in King Chandrasen's royal court.

When King Chandrasen heard what the spies told him, he got very angry. He said, "Take this dacoit and behead him immediately. He has killed a great

scholar and a dear friend, Shridutt. No one can take his place in my life. Oh ! My friend !"

Then the guards took away the dacoit and beheaded him as per the royal order. But that night King Chandrasen

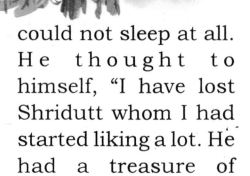

could not sleep at all. He thought to himself, "I have lost Shridutt whom I had started liking a lot. He had a treasure of knowledge. He has died because of me. I am to blame for his death. If I had not given that precious necklace to him, the dacoit would never have killed him to get it. Yes ! I am very sure. I am at fault for all this."

These depressing thoughts set firmly in King Chandrasen's heart and mind. Soon, he became so obsessed with them that he lost interest in everything. He kept blaming himself for Shridutt's death and stopped eating, drinking or sleeping at proper times. All this took its toll and soon he fell very ill. In a few days, King Chandrasen took to the bed and started growing weak.

The queen and the royal ministers tried their best to convince King Chandrasen to stop blaming himself but he felt guilty all the time. The sorry state of health of the king worried the people of Ujjain, too.

One day a scholar visited the royal temple of Ujjain. Everyone had heard of him and he was a great *vaidya* and philosopher, too. The queen and the ministers went to him and told him all about King Chandrasen. At this, the scholar went to meet King Chandrasen in his royal bed-chamber. He talked to the king, "Your Majesty, I have come to know what is ailing you. I think you should stop thinking that you caused Shridutt's death. You are a *Kshatriya*, a warrior who had fought and killed many people in the battle-field, but you never regretted their death. Did you ? Then why now do you blame yourself. After all it was the dacoit who killed Shridutt. By sentencing the dacoit to death, you have done your duty. There is nothing you can do

anymore."

But King Chandrasen still felt depressed. A few thoughtful minutes later the scholar said, "Will you feel better if I use my powers to bring Shridutt to life ?"

King Chandrasen's face lit up with pleasure but a few seconds later he said, "Holy Sir, can you put life back into the dacoit, too ? I'll be highly obliged if you do so."

"No, son, I cannot do so. I have only the limited source of power, so I can bring back to life only one of them." said the scholar to the king.

King Chandrasen grew thoughtful and then he heaved a sigh of regret and said, "If that is the case, I do not want to be a sinner more than I am already. It would be better if Shridutt is not brought back to life."

After completing King Chandrasen's tale, Vetal asked King Vikram, "Now tell me, O just Vikram, wasn't King Chandrasen's behaviour a bit odd ? Why did he refuse for Shridutt's revival to life ? He could have felt better if Shridutt was alive due to the scholar's powers. And why did King Chandrasen ask the dacoit to be brought back to life ? How did King Chandrasen feel he would sin if only Shridutt was made to live once more ? Answer me, King Vikram. But remember, I know it well that you know the right answers to my questions. If you will give the right answers to my questions, I will fly back to my banyan tree. But if you will give me wrong answer even after knowing the correct one, your head will burst into thousand pieces."

To this King Vikram said, "Vetal, I'll tell you the answers to your queries. King Chandrasen was not foolish. He was being a just king. If Shridutt was alive once again then the dacoit's death sentence would be unjust for he was killed as a punishment for taking Shridutt's life.

And if King Chandrasen asked the scholar to use his powers to bring Shridutt to life, then after this the scholar would lose all his powers for this task is of utmost hardship for any scholar to perform. Then the blame of the scholar's lost powers would also be on King Chandrasen and he would become a greater sinner. Having thought of all this, King Chandrasen refused the scholar's offer."

"Yes, Vikram, you are right. Your answer reflects

your intelligence and sense of justice. But you have broken your code of silence. You have spoken up so I am going back to my tree."

With these words, Vetal flew back to the banyan tree.

Suryamukhi

Once again brave King Vikram walked up to the banyan tree, got the corpse and slung it on his shoulder. On the way, Vetal said, "You are a brave and determined man, King Vikram. Now to pass our time I'll tell you a story but you must not speak at all. If you speak, I'll fly back to my home tree. Now here is the story."

Once the prosperous kingdom of Vijaypuri was ruled by a brave, kind and dutiful king named Shivsen. His queen was called Indravati. Many years went by but the couple did not have any child. After a lot of rites and rituals, Queen Indravati gave birth to a beautiful daughter. She was named Suryamukhi.

Great care and attention was paid to Suryamukhi. She was brought up lovingly. Great scholars, warriors and artists were employed to train her in all aspects of life. Though Suryamukhi was a good student at studies but she was inclined towards the classes where she learnt warfare techniques. She proved to be a good horse-woman and could handle all weapons and showed exceptional skill in using swords. Thus, the best teacher in swordsmanship was employed to help the princess to polish her skills.

Years went by and soon Suryamukhi grew into a beautiful maiden. She was now eighteen years of age and queen Indravati was keen on getting her married. When she expressed her thoughts to King Shivsen, he said, "I understand what you feel but I wish to teach the royal duties to my dear daughter, Suryamukhi. I want to make her the ruler of Vijaypuri. I am sure she can be a good ruler for our kingdom. She has all the qualities required for this. I have no regrets that I have no son, for me, my daughter is no less than a son. As for marriage, she can marry a few years from now."

Princess Suryamukhi also liked the idea which her father had. So, on an auspicious day, after certain rituals, the coronation was done and Suryamukhi was crowned as the ruler of Vijaypuri. Under her reign, incidents of thefts and lootings ceased. The unemployed men got jobs in the royal army and the lazy people were taught tough lessons which made them get to work. Help and encouragement from Suryamukhi led to prosperity in agriculture and small industries. Thus, Vijaypuri prospered and King Shivsen's heart was filled with pride.

Two years went by and Queen Indravati again talked to her husband and daughter about her daughter's marriage. This time King Shivsen agreed and so did Suryamukhi. But Suryamukhi said, "Father, please have it announced that I will marry the man who will defeat me in a duel using swords. Only such a man would be my life partner."

Such an announcement was made and kings and princes from many neighbouring kingdoms came to Vijaypuri. Many common men also came to win Suryamukhi's hand in marriage. Then began the

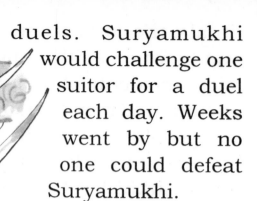

duels. Suryamukhi would challenge one suitor for a duel each day. Weeks went by but no one could defeat Suryamukhi.

The brave prince of Krantipur, Jayant, also heard about the challenge. He dressed up as a common young man and went to the arena in Vijaypuri. For a few days, he watched Suryamukhi's tactics during the duel. Everyday Suryamukhi would win the duel and Jayant would applaud loudly. This had made her notice Jayant. Then Jayant went back to Krantipur and practised well so that he could defeat Suryamukhi. Then one day he dressed up as prince of Krantipur and went for the duel with Suryamukhi. Suryamukhi recognized him instantly. Having known all her tactics, Jayant was able to defeat Suryamukhi.

Then King Shivsen said, "So dear, you have been defeated at last. Are you ready for marriage now?"

To this, Suryamukhi

replied, "No, father, I will not and cannot marry Prince Jayant of Krantipur."

"But why ?" Prince Jayant asked in surprise. "I have completed the challenge you had set."

"Marrying you will be against the law and you know well the reasons for it," said Suryamukhi.

Prince Jayant bowed his head and grew thoughtful. Then he bowed once again with respect to Suryamukhi, "You are correct. I pay my respects to you and take my leave."

Suryamukhi said, "Prince Jayant, I wish you more success in the field of swordsmanship. You may leave now."

Without any word of protest, Prince Jayant left Vijaypuri.

After completing the story, Vetal asked King Vikram, "O great King Vikram, tell me wasn't it unfair of Suryamukhi to reject Prince Jayant even after being defeated by him ? Why did Prince Jayant pay his respects to someone who had rejected him ? What made Suryamukhi wish him good after Prince Jayant had won ? Don't you think it was odd that Prince Jayant accepted all without a protest ? Answer these questions of me. But remember, I know it well that you know the right answers to my questions. If you will give the right answers to my questions, I will fly back to my banyan tree. But if you will give me wrong answer even after knowing the correct one, your head will burst into thousand pieces."

At this King Vikram thought for a few minutes and said, "O Vetal, Suryamukhi was not unfair to Prince Jayant. Prince Jayant had observed all the

Suryamukhi's tactics and learnt from it. In this way, indirectly Suryamukhi had become Jayant's teacher and he had realized this. That is why when she rejected him, he did not protest at all. Suryamukhi clearly knew that marriage between teacher and pupil is against the law.  Jayant also understood this and, thus, paid respects to her as a pupil does to a teacher. In return, Suryamukhi blessed Jayant with luck as a teacher does. So there was no reason for Jayant to feel bad at all."

"King Vikram, your answer reflects your deep understanding of law and dutifulness. I am much impressed but, alas! you have spoken and broken your promise. So here I go back where I came from."

With these words Vetal flew back to the banyan tree. He went and hung on the thick branch just the way King Vikram had found him before.

Dream-Girl

King Vikram was a man who kept his words, so he wanted to fulfill the promise he had made to the monk. Without losing heart, he walked back to the banyan tree. There, he once again saw the corpse hanging on the branch. With great courage, he climbed the tree and took the corpse. Slinging it on his shoulder, he proceeded towards the monk.

Then Vetal spoke up, "You are true to your words, King Vikram. I hope you are doing all this just to keep your promise. Because if you are helping the monk in greed of wealth or beautiful maiden then it's not worth. Let me prove my point to you by telling an old tale. But don't forget, if you speak, I'll go back to the banyan tree once again."

King Manikvarma ruled a rich and happy kingdom of Manidweep. He was an able administrator and all the people in his kingdom were happy and content. After nearly twenty years of marriage King Manikvarma's wife gave birth to a son. The prince was named Sudhir. As he grew up, he was loved and respected by all the people of the kingdom. He was a considerate, law-abiding and righteous young man and had all the good qualities that his father, King Manikvarma had.

By the time, Prince Sudhir came to be twenty years of age, King Manikvarma had grown very old. He was weak in body and mind, too. He used to forget a lot of things so he felt that he was no longer fit to rule Manidweep anymore. The king thought, "Now, I must hand-over my throne to Prince Sudhir. I am sure he will prove to be a good king. But he must, first of all, marry to continue the royal lineage."

So, King Manikvarma enquired about suitable girls to become Prince Sudhir's wife. After some days he decided on getting Prince Sudhir married to Princess Ratnaprabha of Ratnagiri. Showing her picture, the king addressed Prince Sudhir, "Son, look at this beautiful princess. I have chosen her to be your life-partner. Now you must marry her and then take up the responsibilities of Manidweep."

To this, Prince Sudhir bowed respectfully, took the picture and went to his bed-chamber to rest for the night. That night, Prince Sudhir had a dream. In the dream, he saw a beautiful maiden. She was slim and fair, with doe eyes, rosy lips and beautiful, long black hair. She looked at Prince Sudhir lovingly and spread her arms to embrace him and then she disappeared. Prince Sudhir woke up from the dream with a start. The image of the beautiful dream-girl hovered in his heart and mind. He decided that whatever may happen, he will search for her and make her his wife.

Next morning, Prince Sudhir approached King Manikvarma and said, "Father, I have thought about what you said to me last night. Before getting married or becoming the king, I want to tour our kingdom. I want to know how the common people live so as to understand their life-style, their problems and all that goes on outside this protective world of the royal palace. Then I

will have a clear and transparent understanding of the truth of our peoples' lives and that will help me to rule over them better with a view to keep them happy. I think you must give me permission to go on such a tour."

King Manikvarma gave him the permission very happily because he was impressed by his son's thoughts. Without knowing that Prince Sudhir had something else in his mind. Actually, Prince Sudhir wanted to locate his beautiful dream-girl and this plan had sounded good to him.

So the next day, Prince Sudhir dressed as a simpleton and with some food, clothes, a horse and some money left the palace. He roamed around the streets of each city and town in his kingdom. He went to districts and small villages, from temples and mansions to huts and ashrams. He looked for his dream-girl everywhere.

He kept on searching and nearly three months went by with no results at all.

Then he went to some neighbouring kingdoms bordering Manidweep. But even after spending two more months, he still could not find her. With a heavy heart, he started his journey back to Manidweep.

Once on a hot afternoon, Prince Sudhir reached a river. He was tired, therefore he decided to rest for a while. He set his horse free to graze grass growing by the riverside. He himself lay down under a shady tree and was soon asleep. He awoke a few hours later and felt refreshed. He looked around but could not see his horse. He decided to walk on by the river bank to look for his horse. As he walked on, he saw a young maiden sitting on the river bank. Her back was towards prince Sudhir. He approached her and said, "Young lady, have you seen any horse passing by this way ? I had let it free and dozed off. Now I cannot find my horse anywhere."

The young maiden turned to look at Prince Sudhir and oh ! Prince Sudhir stepped back in surprise. His heart-beats increased and his whole body being lit up with joy. Sitting in front of him was the dream-girl, he had been searching for months. Seeing his dream-girl in flesh, made Prince Sudhir overjoyed. He said "Oh ! I have found you. All these months, I have been looking for you everywhere

and here you are atlast. I had seen you in my dreams and I have loved you ever since. Now tell me, will you marry me ? I will always love you and will always be happy."

Such outrageous words from a stranger, scared the young maiden and she ran away. Prince Sudhir ran after her. He soon saw her entering a small, untidy hut by the side of a large rice-field. Immediately, an old man came out of the door of the hut. He looked at Prince Sudhir from head to

toe and then said, "Yes, young man, what do you want? Who are you ? Which village do you belong to? Who are your parents ? You told my daughter that you dreamt of her and you wished to marry her. Do you think it to be a sign of a person belonging to a good family ? Tell me your name, come on, speak up. Answer my questions."

The shower of questions took Prince Sudhir's breath away. He looked hopeless and then in a disappointed tone he said, "I am just a fool !" and that is the answer to all of your questions, sir."

With these words, Prince Sudhir left that place. He

soon found his lost horse and rode back to the capital. In a few days, he reached the royal palace. He was crowned the king of Manidweep and then his marriage was held.

His bride was the beautiful princess of Ratnagiri named Ratnaprabha. Then King Sudhir and Queen Ratnaprabha reigned over Manidweep for many years. He proved himself a just and kind king like his father. He made Manidweep a truly prosperous kingdom than before.

Then Vetal said, "King Vikram, You have heard the story, Prince Sudhir went through so much hardship to search for her dream-girl and then he, at last, found her. But when her father asked him questions, why did he claim to be a fool ? Why did not he tell about himself and marry his dream-girl ? Was he really a fool ? Answer me, King Vikram. But remember, I know it well that you know the right answers to my questions. If you will give the right answers to my questions, I will fly back to my banyan tree. But if you will give me wrong answer even after knowing the correct one, your head will burst into thousand pieces."

Hearing this, King Vikram spoke up. He said, "Prince Sudhir was not a foolish man. But he cannot still be called an intelligent fellow. Seeing a beautiful girl in a dream, he went out to search for her which is something of a waste of time. Only a senseless person would act this way. It was only when the old man questioned him that Prince Sudhir realized his silliness. A simple, common man who wants to get his daughter married enquires a lot about the young man who wishes to marry her. But he, being a prince, never stopped to think and enquire about the girl who he wished to marry and who would hold the responsible and prestigious position of a queen. It should be his duty to enquire about her before acting further. The dream-girl may have been very beautiful

31

indeed but he must first find out if she was fit to be a queen or not. It is not necessary that a beautiful woman would also possess a beautiful nature. To marry her without testing her qualities, would not be sensible. Prince Sudhir realized this when he was faced with the old man's queries. That is why he did not speak much and left for his palace. Then, as a sensible and responsible son and king, he fulfilled all his royal and personal duties."

To this, Vetal said to the king, "Ah ! King Vikram, your answer has warmed my heart. Your understanding of the human nature has been displayed by your very sensible reply.  But now because you have spoken so nothing can stop me from flying back to my favourite tree."

With these words, Vetal flew back to rest on the banyan tree.

True Justice

Without losing heart, King Vikram retraced his determined steps towards the banyan tree. Ignoring the horrifying laughter from the corpse, he reclaimed it and slung it on his shoulder. With a firm determination, he walked towards the direction where the monk was waiting for him.

Vetal spoke once again, "King Vikram, I think you are helping the monk because of some senseless and hasty decision you have taken. Words or oaths taken without thought often lead a man to ruins. To make it clearer, you must listen to this story. But on no account must you speak up or I will fly back to where I belong."

Then Vetal began the story:

In a city named Shivpur, there lived a merchant named Ramanand. He had two sons. Their names were Sudhakar and Dayakar. Sudhakar was a

handsome young man but was not very intelligent. On the other hand, Dayakar had rather ugly features but he was a bright fellow who was learned in all the spheres of business and personal matters.

Once Ramanand's wife fell very ill and soon she passed away. The loss of beloved wife came as a shock to old Ramanand. He, too, fell ill and took to bed. He decided to handover his business to Dayakar. Soon his decision bore sweet fruits as Dayakar used his skills and hard-work to expand the business. In a few months time, Ramanand

was richer than before.

A merchant named Guneshwar also lived in Shivpur. He had two daughters. The elder one was called Rama and the younger one was Shobha. Guneshwar decided that he would get his daughters married to Ramanand's sons. He put his proposal before Ramanand. Ramanand

became very happy with the proposal. Rama was impressed by Sudhakar's handsome looks and she chose him to be her husband. But Shobha refused to marry Dayakar due to his ugly looks. Dayakar grew angry at being rejected. He took an oath and decided, "I will marry a far more beautiful girl than Shobha."

A few weeks later, Sudhakar and Rama were married. Unfortunately, a few days after the ceremony, old Ramanand breathed his last.

One day, Rama went to Dayakar and said, "Dear brother, my sister Shobha rejected your proposal and may be, you are angry with me, too. After all she is my sister. I am scared about our future ?"

"No, Bhabhiji," Dayakar replied, "Have no fears. What can I do to make you feel secure ?"

To this, Rama said, "Just write half of this business and property in your brother's name."

"Why do you ask for half of it ? You can take all of it."

So Dayakar gave all his wealth to his brother. But, as it always happens, having got so much wealth at one go, Rama and Sudhakar became very proud. They did not care for Dayakar anymore. Dayakar realized change in their attitude. He understood well that without money, no person held any importance for others, therefore, he decided to leave home. He went to meet and take leave of his brother and sister-in-law. But Rama requested, "Don't leave home, brother. It is a matter of our prestige. People would think that we banished you from home."

"No, don't worry, dear Bhabhiji," Dayakar said, "You just tell everyone that I gave up all this wealth to you out of kindness. I will use my own skills and power to earn money. I'll come back after becoming a rich man."

With this oath, Dayakar left home. As he walked through a forest, he felt very hungry. He had not eaten for a long time. As he looked around for some fruit-tree, he noticed two men lying on the ground under a shady tree. He approached them. They folded their hands and said, "O stranger, please help us. Dacoits looted all our money and beat us up. We are too hurt and weak to walk. We are also feeling very hungry. Can you give us some food?"

Dayakar looked around and saw a fruit-tree lader with some fruits nearby. He picked all the fruits. Then, making a plate out of some leaves, he offered the fruits to them and said, "Please, eat these fruits. You will surely feel better. Once you have had your fill, please leave some fruits for me to eat for I am hungry, too."

Both of them chewed at the fruits hungrily and ate up all the fruits. Then they felt sorry for having acted this way. Then one of them said, "We are sorry for eating up all the fruits. But we want to pay back for your kind act. My name is Ratnaswami. I am a rich merchant from Bijpur. This is my helper, Kusumakar. Is there anyway we can help you ?"

Dayakar told his story to the merchant Ratnaswami. After hearing his tale of woes, the merchant said, "I have no son to take care of my business. You come and take care of my business."

Dayakar agreed to this and accompanied Ratnaswami and Kusumakar to Bijpur. Dayakar started working in Ratnaswami's shop. While to repay his kindness, Kusumakar let Dayakar stay in his house. Other than a good salary, Ratnaswami also gave shares of his profit to Dayakar. Thus, Dayakar now had some wealth for his future, too.

Kusumakar's beautiful daughter, Manorama, was impressed by Dayakar's intelligence and hard work. She fell in love with him and decided to marry him. On the other hand, Ratnaswami had a rather ugly daughter named Rajwati. Manorama and Rajwati were good friends. Rajwati also had the same feelings and thoughts for Dayakar.

Manorama did not know how to express her love to Dayakar, so she decided to consult that with Rajwati. During the course of conversation, both the friends realized that they both loved Dayakar. So they decided that whoever Dayakar would chose between them, the other would accept it without any ill-feelings.

Back at home Manorama thought, "I am a beautiful girl while Dayakar is a homely fellow. He cannot reject someone as attractive as me. He has taken an oath to marry a beautiful girl, so surely he will accept me as his life-partner."

On the other hand, Rajwati thought, "I am from a rich family and Dayakar is a simple, not so well-off man. He cannot refuse my proposal for he has promised his Bhabhi that he would return after becoming a rich man."

Both the girls told their fathers about their desires to marry Dayakar. Both Ratnaswami and Kusumakar went with the proposals to Dayakar. Dayakar thought for a while and then accepted Ratnaswami's proposal. A few days later, in a grand ceremony, Dayakar married Rajwati.

Vetal then asked, "King Vikram, you must tell me that what made Dayakar reject Manorama. She was a beautiful girl. But he accepted the homely

Rajwati as his wife. Don't you think he married Rajwati for the money? So he kept his oath of getting rich. But what about his oath for marrying a beautiful girl who was better looking than Shobha? Did he not break an oath by doing so? Tell me Vikram. But remember, I know that you know the right answers to my questions. If you will give the right answers to my questions, I will fly back to my banyan tree. But if you will give me wrong answer even after knowing the correct one, your head will burst into thousand pieces."

King Vikram replied to Vetal's questions, "Vetal, Dayakar's decision to marry Rajwati was correct and true justice indeed. He did not marry Rajwati for money. This was apparent that he was not greedy when he gave up his wealth to his brother. His kindness was clearly seen when he fed Ratnaswami and Kusumakar in the forest without eating himself. The same way his decision to marry

Rajwati sprung from the inner good values of his duty and rights that he was aware of. He knew anyone would be ready to marry beautiful Manorama. But homely Rajwati would get a husband who would love her

money but not her. So it would be impossible to get a husband for Rajwati who would love her for the person she was. It was his *dharma* to marry her. His oath to marry a beautiful girl was taken in haste. For such a silly oath, he could not forget his *dharma*. That is why he married Rajwati. Good values and *dharma* ruled his decisions, so it was true justice after all."

"King Vikram, your replies have satisfied me. As always, your answers are full of wisdom. But now that you have spoken, I will go back to my banyan tree." With these words, Vetal flew back to the banyan tree once again.

Dreams Come True

Brave King Vikram went to the banyan tree once again and climbed it. Then he pulled the corpse over his shoulders and walked towards the banyan tree where the monk was waiting for him. But Vetal spoke up, "King Vikram, I can see your firm determination and make out clearly that you are a brave man indeed. But there are times when bravery and skill at war is of no use at all. Those are the times when cleverness and thinking are much more important. Lack of these qualities, can bring to despise any work you had aimed to do. The story, I'll tell you now will make you understand what I want to say."

A long time ago, in Patliputra, there lived a rich merchant called Jayanand. An orphan youth named Vishakh lived with him. As he was the son of a distant relative, Jayanand had let him stay in his house.

Vishakh was a handsome young man, full of intelligence, wit and a treasure of dreams. But he was treated like a servant at the Jayanand's house. He used to keep bemoaning his ill fate. He kept thinking all the time how he could also become rich like Jayanand. He built castles in the air all the time and saw strange dreams at night.

Once in the afternoon, Vishakh was lying and dozing. He dreamt that he had become more richer than Jayanand and Jayanand had become a beggar after having lost all his wealth. Jayanand worked for Vishakh as a servant. In his half asleep state he called out, "Hey Jayanand, you lazy fool ! Where are you ? Come here this minute." By chance Jayanand was passing by the couch. When he heard these words he, lost his temper. He woke up Vishakh and beat him. He threw him out of the grand mansion.

When Jayanand's relatives, maids servants, and neighbours saw Vishakh being treated this way, they made fun of him. Not being able to bear such an insult, Vishakh left Patliputra and walked off to the forest. There, he  saw a hermit meditating under a tree. Vishakh bowed to the hermit with folded hands and paid his respects. The hermit, impressed by this and asked him, "Yes, son, what can I do for you ? Do you think I can help you anyway ?"

Vishakh told the hermit all about what had happened with him in Patliputra and then he requested, "O holy sir ! Please give me powers so that Jayanand falls at my feet and begs for forgive."

Using his powers, the hermit learnt all about Jayanand's past. Then he addressed Vishakh, "Son, Jayanand has earned the high place in the society due to his hardwork and his skills. You are dreaming of becoming a rich man without any hard work. This is like dreaming while you sleep. You must do some work to achieve fame, name and fortune !"

"Holy sir !" said Vishakh. "What you are telling me is nothing new. Everyone says this but if you want to prove that you are a great learned scholar, then you must grant me powers which would make my dreams come true."

The hermit smiled and said, "All right son, I'll do what you want. I will give you a *mantra*. Whenever

you see a dream and you want it to come true, just wake up and chant the *mantra* six times and say aloud that you want your dream to come true. Your wish will be granted. But you must remember that you can use this *mantra* to make only three of your dreams come true. So be careful about for which dream's fulfilment you use the *mantra*."

Then the hermit called Vishakh nearer and recited the *mantra* in his ear. With the knowledge of *mantra* and a new confidence, Vishakh went back to Patliputra. On the way he saw a guest-house and, as it was getting dark, he lay down in its *verandah* and fell asleep. As he slept, he dreamt that Jayanand was apologising to him and he was also offering his only beautiful daughter's hand in marriage to him. Vishakh woke up with a start and decided to test the hermit's *mantra*. So Vishakh recited the *mantra* six times and wished that his dream must come true. A few minutes later, he heard the sound of pipes and drums. He looked around and saw Jayanand leading a band of musicians towards Vishakh. He came and stopped near Vishakh and said, "Son, forgive me for the way I treated you. Please, come back home. I wish to marry my daughter Malini to a worthy, handsome young boy like you. Please accept this proposal to prove that you have forgiven me."

Vishakh accepted the proposal instantly and then went home with Jayanand. Vishakh's dream came true and amidst a grand arrangements of music, lights, flowers and decorations, Vishakh wed beautiful Malini. Now Vishakh led a luxurious and happy life in Jayanand's house. Jayanand treated him well for he was his son-in-law now. But the servants, maids, relatives and neighbours of Jayanand could not take this. They did not accept the fact that an idle youth who was once treated like a servant, was now like the master of the house. Both Vishakh and Jayanand observed the jealous peoples' attitude. So Jayanand said, "Vishakh, people are jealous as they think that I am giving all the comforts to you for free. You must prove yourself to them. I will give you some money. You must start your own business, work hard and become a prosperous and rich man."

Vishakh agreed to this. That night, Vishakh had a dream in which his business prospered and expanded in three months' time. He was respected as one of the richest merchants of Patliputra. Vishakh woke up and then he called Malini. He told her about the dream. She said, "Oh ! It's only a dream and you know very well that dreams never come true. Come on, let us go back to sleep."

But Vishakh told Malini all about the hermit's *mantra*. Then, to prove it to her, Vishakh recited the *mantra* six times and prayed that his dream must come true. Next morning, he went to work as usual and was

flooded by orders for

trade. And, within three months' time, Vishakh became a very rich merchant and was respected by the people of Patliputra.

As days went by, Vishakh became a millionaire but this good news entailed some problems, too. His competitors started spreading a rumour that Vishakh was selling adulterated products. Some started saying that by meddling with his accounts he showed less than his actual profits to avoid paying income-tax and other royal taxes. By doing this, he was cheating both the king and the public of Patliputra. Soon enough, the king of Patliputra, heard these rumours, too. A case was filed in the royal court and the king summoned Vishakh. He said, "Vishakh, I have heard that you have avoided paying taxes and have hoarded a lot of money. You must now pay ten times the royal tax amount within ten days time. If you do not do so, you will have to face seven years imprisonment."

Vishakh had never faced a more difficult situation than this one. As ill luck would have it, his father-in-law Jayanand fell ill and passed away within a few days. Thus, Vishakh had no one to guide him or advise him in such difficult times.

One night, when Vishakh was sleeping, he dreamt that he had become the king of Patliputra and was punishing his competitors for spreading false rumours about him. Vishakh woke up and told Malini about the dream he had seen. Malini exclaimed in happiness, "Oh, dear, it's such a wonderful dream. If you become the king of Patliputra, you won't have to pay any taxes. You would be able to punish the meddling competitors and we would have a grand, luxurious life with nothing to worry about. Now you must recite the hermit's *mantra* and make this

dream come true."

But Vishakh grew silent and thoughtful. He told Malini that he was going to meet the hermit and left for the forest. He went and bowed to the hermit and said, "Holy sir, I do not want to use the *mantra* for the third time. Please take away the power of *mantra* from me."

The hermit smiled and said, "I did not think that your heart will be lit by the light of knowledge so soon. I hereby make the *mantra* powerless. Now you are free of its power. You may go now."

Vishakh went back to Patliputra and sold off all his property. He paid the royal taxes as per order of the king. Then, with a small amount of money, he left for a small town with Malini. There in the town, he started a small business and was content with what he earned. So, he and Malini led the rest of their lives full of joy and contentment.

Then Vetal asked, "King Vikram, the story is over.

Vishakh could have made his dream come true and become a king. He lost a golden chance to punish his competitors. Wasn't he foolish for not using his *mantra* for the third time ? Can you tell me why Vishakh behaved in such a way ? But remember, I know it well that you know the right answers to my questions. If you will give the right answers to my questions, I will fly back to my banyan tree. But if you will give me wrong answer even after knowing the correct one, your head will burst into thousand pieces."

After a few thoughtful moments, King Vikram said, "If all our dreams come true then life would not be interesting at all. Joys and sorrows, success and failures, lend a beautiful hue to our life. Other than this, it's the fruits of hardwork that taste sweet. If all our dreams come true then there would be no importance of hardwork and people, who want to earn respect with hardwork, could not achieve their aim. And that was the only thing which the hermit wanted Vishakh to learn in life. When he gained the position of a rich son-in-law without any hard work, he became

51

the target of jealousy. The same way he became a millionaire without working hard for it and also became the target of his competitors' ill feelings. The hermit's *mantra* could make his dreams come true but could do nothing to help him to face the entailing problems. If he had become a king, he would have punished the other merchants and had a fine life. But, along with this, he would have to carry out the duties and responsibilities of a king. To handle a large kingdom and its people, one needs special qualities and skills which he lacked. This realization made Vishakh go to the hermit to make the *mantra* powerless."

Vetal said, "Yes, Vikram ! Your answer is what I had expected. You have read into Vishakh's mind and thoughts. But now that you have spoken I am flying away."

And Vetal flew back to the banyan tree.

King Satyapal

King Vikram approached the banyan tree once again. He climbed up the tree, took the hanging corpse, slung it on his shoulder and walked on.

The Vetal addressed King Vikram, "King Vikram, a king like you shows how important hardwork and determination are for a king to rule his kingdom. But, along with this, a king must also have ample knowledge of administration and political prowess. Let me prove it to you by this tale."

A long time ago, Chandandesh was ruled by King Chandrapal. Once he fell very ill and breathed his last. His son, Prince Satyapal, now took over the royal throne. In a few days after coronation, Satyapal realized the bad situation of the country. He understood that his father had just lived to enjoy the luxurious life of a king. He had given over all the royal administrative

responsibilities to ministers and officials. They, in turn, were exploiting the people by levying heavy taxes and taking bribes. They had all hoarded money through illegal means.

Other than these internal problems, King Satyapal was also deeply troubled by problems from his neighbouring kingdoms. On the eastern border of Chandandesh was a country ruled by Bhils. For centuries, they had been subject to the general rule of Chandandesh.

Spies had informed King Satyapal that the Bhil king, Jayasen, had been planning to wage a war to gain independence. Another neighbouring country bordering Chandandesh and the country of Bhils was Mihirdesh. It was ruled by King Prachandverma. He knew all about the internal problems of Chandandesh and, using them as an advantage, he wanted to occupy Chandandesh. This information had reached King Satyapal's ears through his spies.

Facing so many problems, King Satyapal was getting worried a lot. So, one day he summoned his

Prime Minister, Kewal Bhatt to discuss the situation. Kewal Bhatt said, "Your Majesty, we must first deal with the problems outside our country. We can take care of our internal problems later on. If the external problems continue, then our enemies will attack and occupy our kingdom. There is only one solution to all this."

"Yes, what is it ?" King Satyapal encouraged.

Kewal Bhatt said, "Your Majesty, you should marry Madhulika, the princess of Mihirdesh. She is King Prachandverma's daughter. This way your conflict with them will be over and you will have extra strength in case Bhils attack us."

"But Prachandverma is our enemy. He will never agree to this," King Satyapal said.

Prime Minister, Kewal Bhatt said, "Your Majesty, the spies have told me that Madhulika, likes you a lot and wants to be your queen. I think we must send her a secret message that you feel the same for her."

"But my spies have said that she is a very proud girl!" King Satyapal interrupted.

"Yes, Your Majesty. But she is very young. Once she gets married and becomes a queen, she will start behaving like a mature lady."

But King Satyapal did not reply. He kept thinking of some ways to solve the problems.

At last, King Satyapal decided to visit his guru's ashram in Kanchangiri. As he was passing through the forest, suddenly a cheetah attacked King Satyapal's horse. The horse panicked and started running at a fast pace. The horse kept running and King Satyapal could not control it. After a few minutes, King Satyapal heard a strange sound. The horse stopped running and calmed down. King Satyapal realized that it had been a sound made by a Bhil youth. They used such a sound to control frightened horses. King Satyapal looked around and observed that he had reached

the forest which bordered the Bhil country. Then, a young Bhil boy came in front of King Satyapal. He asked the boy, "Were you the one who made the sound ?"

"Yes," the youth replied, "You look tired. You must rest a while now. I'll be back in a few minutes."

Hearing the young Bhil's voice, King Satyapal had some suspicion in his mind. He smiled to himself and sat under the tree. A few moments later, the

young Bhil returned with some fruits and water. King Satyapal said to him, "Thank you for helping me. Come to my kingdom and I will give you a job that befits you."

"No, I have only done my duty. I don't want anything in return. I am leaving."

Hearing this, King Satyapal grew enraged and said, "How can you say so ? Don't you know you are talking to the king of Chandandesh ? You are a citizen of a dependent country."

Then the youth said, "I know you have recognised

me. I am Kirtisena, King Jayasen's daughter. You were trying to provoke me to reveal my true identity."

King Satyapal laughed and said, "You were trying to talk in a heavy voice like men but I made out that you were acting. All right, Princess Kirtisena, I'll take your leave."

But the Princess said, "Please stop ! Will you come with me ?"

King Satyapal followed Princess Kirtisena to a statue. Princess Kirtisena bowed before it and said, "I will wait for you near this statue exactly two months from now. She is Devi Swayamshakti Mata. Seek her blessings and all your problems will be solved soon."

King Satyapal offered prayers to the statue and went back to Chandandesh. There he ordered

the arrest of all corrupt ministers and officials and claimed their wealth and property which he transferred to the royal treasury. Then he ordered that all the troops must be trained well once again and their salaries increased. All tax evaders, bribe-takers and anti-social elements were arrested and put in prison. Chandandesh now progressed towards prosperity.

Two months went by. King Satyapal went to meet Kirtisena in the forest. He went to the statue and waited for her. Kirtisena arrived soon enough. Seeing her, King Satyapal said, "With blessings of Swayamshakti Mata all my problems have been solved. Now I am free of my country's internal problems. Will you now agree to marry me and be my queen?"

Kirtisena felt shy to reply but she bowed her head in acceptance. She went back to the palace and told all this to her father, the Bhil king. He in turn sent gifts to King Satyapal with the proposal for marriage. King Satyapal happily accepted the proposal and he was married to Princess Kirtisena in a grand ceremony. Then, with the added strength of Bhil army, King Satyapal attacked Mihirdesh and conquered King Prachandverma.

After the defeat, King Prachandverma said, "I have no regrets about losing my kingdom or throne but I worry for my daughter, Madhulika. King Satyapal, will you marry her and make her your queen ? Only then I will be free of all my responsibilities."

King Satyapal agreed and soon he was married to Princess Madhulika. So Madhulika became the second queen of Chandandesh. Mihirdesh also became Chandandesh's dependent. Thus, King Satyapal solved both his internal and external problems and led a fine married life with his new bride.

Then Vetal asked, "King Vikram, tell the answers to my queries. King Satyapal cleansed and polished the corrupt administration of

60

Chandandesh. He did not have the knowledge of political dealings and treatment given to other kings. He acted in a childish manner. This became clear in the way he proposed to Kirtisena and how he was not able to express his feelings for Madhulika. Both King Chandrapal and King Satyapal were not working for their country. Don't you think so? Tell me the answers to my questions. But remember, I know it well that you know the right answers to my questions. If you will give the right answers to my questions, I will fly back to my banyan tree. But if you will give me wrong answer even after knowing the correct one, your head will burst into thousand pieces."

To this King Vikram replied, "Whatever King Satyapal did from the moment he was crowned king, to his marriage with Madhulika, all the actions were correct. He ignored Kewal Bhatt's words and dealt with internal matters before paying attention to the external matters of his country. He did not lack political prowess. For a king it is most necessary to win the trust of his own people before tackling the enemies. This is his true strength. King Satyapal knew  this and that's why he first arrested the corrupt officials. Bhil king wanted independence but did not want to attack or occupy like the king of Mihirdesh. Kirtisena made her love clear to him by taking him to the Devi's statue. King Satyapal did not want a proud wife like Madhulika so, he proposed to Kirtisena. Madhulika had not expressed her feelings due to her pride. May be, she thought that her father would defeat King Satyapal and gift him to her. These thoughts made King Satyapal prefer Kirtisena to Madhulika. He merely used his political prowess by accepting Prachandverma's proposal. He used his political prowess to turn the events to his advantage."

By answering Vetal, King Vikram had broken his promise so Vetal flew back to the banyan tree again.

Ugrashil's Tale

King Vikram went again to the banyan tree possessed by Vetal and climbed up. He took the corpse on his shoulders and climbed down. King Vikram went towards the banyan tree under which the monk was waiting him, with determination.

Vetal spoke up once again. He said, "King Vikram, I know people work hard to earn money or to gain prosperity in life. But I wonder why are you working hard here at the middle of the night? Some kings are not as intelligent as you are. They are foolish and take hasty decisions. They carry out whatever comes to their mind without thinking of the consequences. I'll tell you about such a king who made a hasty decision regarding a fierce dacoit."

Once a king named Satyendra ruled over Manikarnika. In the dense forests of the country,

there lived a fierce and ruthless dacoit named Ugrashil. He lived in a cave located in the centre of the deep, dense forest. He had a huge gang comprising about fifty dacoits. They would go to distant villages at night and rob the people of their cash and ornaments. The people knew that the leader of that huge gang of dacoits was named Ugrashil. But no one recognised him or his dacoits. This was because each time they went to loot some villages, they would have their faces covered.

Sometimes, the gang would go to loot distant villages and it would take nearly four to five days to go and come back to the cave. During this period, Ugrashil's wife would worry for her husband's safety. Many a times, she had tried to convince her husband that he should give up the life of a dacoit. She wanted to have a fearless life of a simple man's wife. But Ugrashil would say, "Dear, it's too late now. Now I am a dacoit and I cannot change my calling, this way."

After a few years, Ugrashil's wife gave birth to a healthy baby boy. Ugrashil loved his son very much. He loved to play with the tiny baby's hands. The baby's smile and gurgling voice would fill his heart with love and joy. Gradually, Ugrashil's nature softened. He used to speak gently and his way of looting became less cruel. On a looting merriment if he happened to get into a house and see children there, he would start kissing them. He would play with them before leaving with the loot. Other dacoits warned him, "Sir, if you continue like this, someday we will surely be caught. We must always be quick to loot and leave. You must not

spend time with children this way."

But try as he might, Ugrashil could not revert himself to his former cruel, heartless nature. One day, as he had gone to loot a far away village, he felt tired on the way. He and his dacoits stopped to rest for a while. Ugrashil lay in the shade of a tree and dozed off. Then he saw a dream that he was riding his horse. As the horse was running fast, it stumbled and fell. Ugrashil also fell off the horse.

When he got up, he saw king's soldiers chasing him. As he ran, one of them threw a spear that pierced his back. The next instant he saw his wife and baby boy falling down into a deep gorge. Ugrashil woke up from sleep with a start. He dreaded that his dream might come true in the future.

Ugrashil woke up the dacoits and said, "I think we all must leave this sinful way of life. I am thinking of going to the king and surrendering. All of you must think about it and tell me by tomorrow morning."

Then he led the dacoits back to the cave and told his wife about his decision. His wife was surprised by her husband's sudden decision of surrendering. But she was happy anyway. On the other hand, the wives of his dacoits were surprised to see their husbands returning without any loot. When they asked about the matter, the dacoits made up some false tales to avoid answering. Next morning, Ugrashil called his dacoits and said, "If we surrender, the king will be gentle in punishing us. We must all think about our children. If we stay as dacoits, we cannot give our children a safe, educated and decent future."

The dacoits did not feel the way Ugrashil did. They all refused to surrender. That night Ugrashil could not sleep. As he went out of the cave for a walk, he heard two of his dacoits talking, "Since the birth of the child our leader has become soft in his heart and head. His plan of surrendering is foolish. I think we must kill his wife and son to teach him a lesson."

Hearing this, Ugrashil felt scared for his wife's and son's life. So he came back to his cave. He woke up his wife and son and decided to leave the forest. He took his horse, some clothes and money along with them and left the forest. In the dark of the night,

they reached the capital city. Ugrashil thought that he would use the money to start a small business but he feared that some day or the other, his identity would be revealed.

In the midnight, he reached the palace. He evaded the royal guards and entered the king's private bed chamber. As he got into his bed chamber through the window, his hand struck a vase in the dark. There was a loud noise and the king woke screaming, "Thief ! Thief ! Guards, where are you?"

As the guards entered the chamber, Ugrashil said, "No, Your Majesty, I am not a thief. I am here to meet you."

"Guards, search him first," the king ordered.

When the guards searched him, they found no weapons or tools used by thieves. So the king ordered, "Guards, you may leave now."

"Yes, who are you ? What made you come to meet me this way ?" the king enquired.

"Your Majesty, my name is Ugrashil. I am the leader of the notorious gang of dacoits. I am here to surrender because....." and Ugrashil told all about himself and his decisions to the king. The king heard him out with great patience and understanding. Then the king took a bag full of a hundred gold coins and while giving it to Ugrashil, he said, "Take this money and go to start a business. Exactly after one year, you come to me with double of this amount. But you must double that money with hard-earned money only. Now you are free to leave my country and go anywhere to start a new life, but you must return in a year as promised."

Then the king summoned the guards and said, "Lead this man respectfully and leave him and his family on the highway that borders our country."

Thus, Ugrashil left with his wife and son for another country.

Vetal then asked King Vikram, "King Vikram, when Ugrashil had come to surrender himself, why did the king let him go ? Why did King Satyendra not punish him ? On the other hand, he gave Ugrashil hundred gold coins to start a

business. Don't you think that this was a hasty decision by him ? Did he have any proof that Ugrashil was being truthful and would return a year later ? How could the king be sure that Ugrashil would not rob or loot again in the future ? The king could have given him a job in the palace to keep an eye on him. Why, do you think, he let the dacoit go free ? Even if we believe that Ugrashil had changed, then what about his gang members ? I think King Satyendra did not think before he acted. Clear my confused thoughts. But remember, I know it well that you know the right answers to my questions. If you will give the right answers to my questions, I will fly back to my banyan tree. But if you give me wrong answer even after knowing the correct one, your head will burst into thousand pieces."

To this, King Vikram replied, "Vetal, King Satyendra gave an example of his intelligence and kind-heartedness by letting Ugrashil free to lead a simple life. The aim of punishment is to make the culprit realize his mistake and bring changes in his life.

Ugrashil had already gone through these changes. By giving him money, the king had set a challenge for Ugrashil to lead an honest life, which is more tougher than going through physical punishment for him. The fact that Ugrashil came to surrender inspite of his gang members' refusal to accompany him, shows that he was determined to lead an honest life. The king knew where Ugrashil's dacoits were hiding, so he could send his army to arrest them. Otherwise, the dacoits after knowing the king's kind and lenient attitude towards their leader, also surrender themselves. These basic, logical and sensible conclusions were reached upon by King Satyendra before he let Ugrashil leave the country. So I think his decision was not hasty at all."

"King Vikram," Vetal said. "You are able to impress me each time we meet. Your sense of justice is great. But here you have spoken and thus, I will take my flight back to the tree."

Fruits of Jealousy

King Vikram went back and climbed up the banyan tree once again. He pulled the corpse and started to walk on towards the monk waiting for him. In the way, Vetal said, "King Vikram, why are you trying so hard to hand over me to the monk ? Why are you doing this anyway ? If it is out of a feeling of jealousy or competitiveness, then I assure you that you will gain nothing out of it. I'll tell you a story to make my point clearer to you."

A long time ago, there was a rich land-owner named Chakrabhupati. He owned nearly two third of a village. He had a loyal and honest servant named Gopal who had been serving him for many years. Chakrabhupati had a lot of wealth and a lovely wife, but he had no children. Gopal was living a comfortable life on the salary he received. He also had a devoted wife but no children. This had made Chakrabhupati and Gopal share the same sorrow, that had bonded them together like friends.

Once a great sage came to a neighbouring village. He was well known as the one who helped the needy, through his miracles. Chakrabhupati heard of the sage and went to meet him with his wife. There he offered fruits and some gifts to the sage and told him about his problems. The sage performed a prayer and then gave a *taveej* (magic powered locket) to Chakrabhupati's wife. He said, "Go and perform prayer to Lord Shiva for forty-five days and then wear this *taveej*. Your wishes will be fulfilled."

Gopal also visited the mahatma with his wife and received the *taveej*.

After a couple of months, both the women conceived and as luck would have it, both of them delivered healthy baby boys. Chakrabhupati and Gopal were overwhelmed with joy. The rich land-owner arranged a grand feast for all the villagers.

As years went by, Chakrabhupati's son Kamal and Gopal's son Chandar grew up together. Teachers came home to teach Kamal everyday but he showed little interest in studies. The love he received for being the only child and the fulfilment

of all his wishes had made him very stubborn and disobedient. On the other hand, Gopal's love and little means had made Chandar an intelligent boy. He understood his family's conditions and never made unnecessary demands to his parents. He went to the village school and was a brilliant student who topped in class, each year.

All these years, Chakrabhupati had observed the progress made by Chandar. The failures and spoilt nature of his own son, Kamal, had made him sad. Each time he saw Chandar, he would feel jealous of Gopal for having such a good son. Few years later, it was time for the boys to go for higher studies. So, one day when Gopal went to Chakrabhupati to ask for money to send Chandar to Kashi for higher studies, he refused point blank. Gopal went home with a heavy heart and said, "Chandar, my son, I could not arrange money to send you to the university in Kashi. Please forgive me."

Chandar understood his father's problem and decided to forego his desires for further studies.

Chakrabhupati was worried because of his problems. He did not sleep at nights. He felt sorry for having a useless son like Kamal who did not want to study or progress in life. His love for his only son stopped him from scolding him. He kept all his worries to himself and soon became a short-tempered person. He would got irritated at small matters. His family members and workers did not know that his feelings of jealousy for Chandar had brought this change in him.

One evening, Chakrabhupati saw Chandar and Kamal talking in a fruit orchard. He went and hide behind a nearby tree and heard their conversation.

Kamal was saying, "Chandar, I have heard your father was approached by the headmaster. He asked your father to send you to Kashi for further 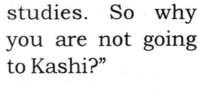 studies. So why you are not going to Kashi?"

Chandar replied calmly, "But friend, why are you putting pressure on me to do so? Give me one good reason for it. My father has decided to send me for

further studies. He has said that he will approach your father for money once again and your kind father will surely help him."

"But Chandar, why do you want to study on borrowed money ? You must drop the idea of going to Kashi. I will give you some money for now and you can look for a good job here." Kamal said to Chandar.

"I need money for further studies. If I cannot study then I don't need the money at all. For me, studies are more important," said Chandar.

Kamal felt irritated by Chandar's insulting refusal and walked away without a word.

Chakrabhupati had heard and seen all. He felt happy in his heart. Then he went home and summoned Gopal. When Gopal came to him, Chakrabhupati said, "Take these three thousand rupees and send Chandar to Kashi for studies today itself. If you need more money, you can ask for it. You don't have to spend any money for his studies. I'll pay for Chandar's further education."

Gopal received the money thankfully and went off

to give the good news to Chandar. The next day Chandar left for Kashi to study and become a learned scholar. Chakrabhupati saw his progress in studies and felt very happy.

Vetal asked King Vikram, "King Vikram, what brought the sudden change in Chakrabhupati's behaviour ? Do you think it was after seeing Chandar's determination to study or it was because Gopal strongly felt that he would surely give money for his son's education ? The trust reposed in him by Gopal may be a reason, don't you think so? While Chakrabhupati was depressed on seeing Kamal's lack of interest in studies then how could he be so enthusiastic about someone else's son's studies ? Will you help me to clear the confusion ? But remember, I know it well that you know the right answers to my

questions. If you give the right answers to my questions, I will fly back to my banyan tree. But if you will give me wrong answer even after knowing the correct one, your head will burst into thousand pieces?"

At this, King Vikram said, "The truth became clear before Chakrabhupati when he heard the conversation between Chandar and Kamal. He realized that Kamal was very jealous of Chandar's studies and progress. A person feels jealous only when a desire to progress has taken birth in his heart. Chakrabhupati understood that the same feeling to progress has now taken place in Kamal's mind. The spirit to succeed and to compete was clearly visible in Kamal's attitude. This would surely lead to his successful progress. Another thing was that the Kamal's jealousy was on a very small level that is

why Chandar's determination could not be shaken by Kamal's jealous words. Kamal had left without arguing much. He had decided not to bother Chandar anymore. Kamal's jealousy was what fellow students felt for competing in studies and this would urge Kamal to study harder to fare better than Chandar. Seeing this change in Kamal, had made Chakrabhupati very happy. To encourage Kamal more, indirectly, he had decided to help Chandar. It had nothing to do with Gopal's trust in him or Chandar's feelings towards further education."

Vetal heard this explanation and said, "Ah ! The great learned Vikram, you have cleared my mind of all confusions. I fully agree to your views. But you have spoken, so I will now take your leave."

With these words, once again Vetal flew back to his banyan tree.

Devta Kusum

Without any hitch, King Vikram retraced his steps back to the banyan tree. Climbing up the branches, he pulled the corpse to his shoulder. Then he started to walk to the monk.

But once again, Vetal spoke up. He said, "King Vikram, you are taking pains to take me to the monk. Are you doing all this to gain some magical powers that keep you forever young ? If you are doing all this to achieve this aim then let me assure you that there are no such powers. And if they do exist then they are just not fit for humans. To make this clear to you, I'll tell an interesting story to you. Please be kind enough to listen carefully."

A long time ago, the kingdom of Vyjantpur was ruled by King Anantvarma. He had grown very old and he had no children. He always worried as who would takeover the throne after him. He always kept thinking of this because he felt that the days of his life were numbered.

Once, on a full moon night, King Anantvarma was strolling on the roof of his palace. His minister Chandragupta, was with him. Suddenly, the king said, "See Chandragupta, how beautiful this moonlit night is! The fragrant flowers in my garden, this grand palace, I will soon leave these and go to heaven."

Chandragupta was speechless when he heard such words. The next moment a strange thing happened. A beautiful flower fell at the king's feet. It was a golden flower. The king picked up the delicate flower with surprise. He smelt it and said, "Oh! Chandragupta, this is such a wonderful flower. I cannot describe the heavenly fragrance that it emanates."

"Your Majesty," Chandragupta said, "I think it is Kusum Dev. Some divine maiden must be passing by in the sky and this flower has fallen off her hair. There must be something behind this incident. We must consult the Royal priest about this."

Next morning King Anantvarma summoned the Royal priest and showed him the flower. After hearing about how the king had got it, the Royal priest said, "Your Majesty, this is the favoured flower of the divine maidens in heavens, called Amritavardhani. This flower is used by great *Ayurveda* practitioners. According to them, if any young man or woman prays to the god and smells this flower and then intends to give away his youth to some old person, then this flower can fill old people with the energy and jest of youth. But this flower can provide youth to only one person. So the one, who gains from it, will be exceptionally lucky."

Hearing these words, King Anantvarma danced with joy. He turned to Chandragupta and said, "Let it be announced all over the kingdom that the young man, who gifts his youth to the king, will get half the kingdom along with a large number of precious gifts."

So announcement about that had been made all over the kingdom.

Chandragupta knew that the king was doing this to have a son of his own. A week later Chandragupta led some soldiers

outside the capital city. He saw two beggars near a temple. One of them was blind and the other one was suffering from a skin disease. Chandragupta approached them and said, "A week ago, a royal message had been announced all over the kingdom. Did you hear about it ? His Majesty has said that whosoever gifts his youth to him will receive half of the kingdom and many precious gifts. Come forward and accept this offer. It will change your life for sure."

But both the beggars showed no reaction or excitement at all. This made Chandragupta very angry. He asked once again, "The king will give you half of his kingdom, won't you like that ?" The blind beggar said, "Sir, I am blind. What is the use of half or even the whole kingdom for me ? I cannot see or enjoy its pleasures."

Then the second beggar replied, "Sir, I could have given my youth to the king but, alas ! What would I do if I have to enjoy the pleasures as an old man. I am already troubled with this skin disease. Adding old age to the list of my woes, will be too much a burden to carry."

Chandragupta grew irritated by this reply. In disgust, he left both the beggars to look for some other young man. As luck would have it, no one in the kingdom was ready to give away his youth. Everyone had some tale to refuse the offer. At last Chandragupta got tired of searching and headed back for the royal palace.

A few days later, Chandragupta and the soldiers reached the capital. They went directly to the royal court. The royal court was in session. King Anantvarma was sitting on the throne. He was busy listening to the case of the notorious dacoit Ram Singh. The dacoit was a young man of about twenty years of age. Ram Singh was speaking. He was saying, "Your Majesty, I did not loot people indiscriminately. I robbed the corrupt people of the capital city who had hoarded their wealth by taking bribes. I have kept only a small amount for myself. All the remainder of my loots have been distributed amongst the poor and the needy. I never looted or insulted any woman. Even when it came to self-defence, I never took anyone's life."

It was apparent from the honest tone of his voice that Ram Singh was telling the truth. King Anantvarma was pleased with his honesty but he knew that after all Ram Singh was a notorious dacoit. The king had to punish the dacoit for his misdeeds but he was also impressed by his honesty and was in double mind about his decision.

Before the king could speak further, Chandragupta went to him. He whispered in his ear, "Your Majesty, I went all around the kingdom. I even met some beggars but I could not find anyone who would gift his youth to you. I have some hope from this young dacoit. Please grant me permission to ask him in my own way."

The king nodded his approval. So Chandragupta went to dacoit Ram Singh and said, "For all the

misdeeds and robberies that you have committed, we can easily sentence you to death but......, I think...."

But before the minister could say anything, the dacoit Ram Singh interverned. He said, "But you think that I must gift my youth to the king. Then I will be allowed to live and rule half of this kingdom. Isn't this what you intended to ask me ?"

Chandragupta was amazed at the dacoit's intelligence. He said, "Yes, you have guessed right. Now tell me do you agree to accept this offer?"

In reply, dacoit Ram Singh laughed aloud. He said, "Your Majesty, I would be thankful at the bottom of my heart if you decide to forgive my sins. And if you decide to punish me according to the law of our kingdom, then too, I would be proud of you for being our just king. But if none of this happens, then my heart will be heavy with regrets for all my guesses would fall false. I had heard the royal announcement and had deliberately let myself be caught by the royal guards. I had all intentions of gifting my youth to you but now I have changed my mind. I see that selfishness is at the forefront here. If any task is motivated by selfishness then I feel it is the lowest tasks of all. I am sorry to say this, but Your Majesty, I can see selfishness guiding you at this very moment."

Hearing such insulting words, King Anantvarma lost his temper. He shouted, "Having heard of your cruel acts, I will direct my guards to hang you this very minute."

But Ram Singh calmly replied, "If you think this to be a fit punishment for me then go ahead with it. But please be assured that your threats of punishment won't make me accept your minister's offer. If you think you can scare me or threaten me to say 'yes' then you are absolutely wrong."

The confidence with which dacoit Ram Singh spoke, impressed the King Anantvarma's mind. Suddenly, the knowledge shone brightly in his mind and he realized his mistake. His face grew red with shame. He sat still for a few moments and then he grew calm. He got up from the throne and approached dacoit Ram Singh and embraced him. Then

the king said, "Son, you have enlightened my soul and made me realize my misthoughts with your words. You are great. To have met an intelligent and learned person like you is an honour to me. I have no heir to my throne. Now, at this very moment, I declare you to be my succesor. Now I will go to the forest and become a hermit."

After ending the tale, Vetal enquired of King Vikram, "King Vikram, now please answer my queries. In his old age, was it not utterly disgusting of King Anantvarma to nurture such thoughts of youth? Was it right to embrace and enthrone a notorious criminal this way? But what made the king to decide about becoming a hermit? Can you make all this clear to me ? Answer me soon. But remember, I know it well that you have the right answers to my questions. If you will give the right answers to my questions, I will fly back to my banyan tree. But if you will give me wrong answer even after knowing the correct one, your head will burst into thousand pieces."

After a few thoughtful moment, King Vikram replied, "From Anantvarma's behaviour it is clear

that he was a cultured, nature-loving and art-loving person. This was his true nature but somehow he had been swept away by emotions and had grown weak. To call this momentary weakness of thoughts as being foolish or indecent is absolutely incorrect. This is a fact that the desire of youth made Anantvarma forget this, momentarily. The confidence and fearlessness displayed by Ram Singh in expressing his thoughts, enlightened Anantvarma. He saw how the dacoit was not having any desire to save himself. This cultured attitude and sense of sacrifice made the dacoit great in the king's eyes. This motivated him to give up the throne to the dacoit. Anantvarma realized that death was sure to come. That's why, he accepted it willingly and calmly decided to become a hermit for his own peace of mind."

At King Vikram's reply, Vetal said, "Once again you have proved yourself to me. But now you have spoken and I'll leave you here."

With these words, Vetal flew back to settle on his home tree.

The Selfish Merchant

King Vikram traced his steps back to the banyan tree of Vetal. Reclaiming the corpse, he started to walk towards the banyan tree where the monk was waiting for him.

Vetal spoke again. He said, "King Vikram, I see that you are taking great pains to complete this task. Are you sure that can achieve this aim in your

lifetime ? Actually many people keep thinking of desires or aims that cannot be fulfilled by them. And then, when they fail to do so, they do not realize these follies. They do not possess the logical thinking or knowledge of human nature that would help them achieve their aims. That's why they feel defeated when they fail and don't know what to do next. At such times, they start to depend on their offsprings to fulfill their desires and sadly, they sometimes face failures yet again. To make you understand what I want to convey, you must pay attention to the story that I am about to tell you."

And then Vetal began to tell this story :

A long time ago, a rich merchant Dhangupta lived in Bhagyanagar. He was good in his trade and business. He used to help anyone who approached him. He respected and loved his relatives very

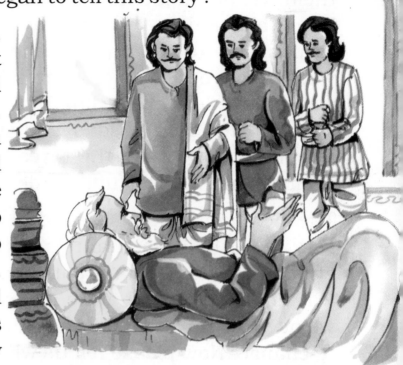

much. Being a simple and helpful man, he never realized that he had been taken advantage of. All his relatives were selfish. They used to tell some painful story to him and take some help or money from him. Years went by like this, and one day Dhangupta realized the truth. But by then it was too late because he had grown very old.

Dhangupta had three sons. They were named Anand, Vinod and Vivek. One day Dhangupta summoned all of them and said, "Dear sons, I want to tell you something important. If you want to get involved in my business then along with ability to work, you must have a streak of selfishness. I did not have that quality. That is why my relatives and friends benefitted from me. They took me to be a fool and kept taking advantage of me. Now, I have realized that I have suffered a lot of losses due to them. We are millionaires now, but we could have been billionaires. In a way all of you are responsible for my present financial status. If it was not for you, I would not even be a millionaire. I would have lost everything by now. I know all of you are my dutiful sons and are very good at business. Now, I ask the three of you to make a promise that you will fulfil my desire."

The merchant's elder son said, "Father, we know it very well that merchants must have a selfish streak in them. Actually path that you treaded on was not liked by us but we respected you a lot, so we never commented or made any requests to you to change. Now please tell us what you desire. We shall surely fulfil your desire."

Dhangupta was pleased at such a reply from his sons. He said, "Many people have told me that my business could have been even better but the house I live in is very unlucky. Its bad

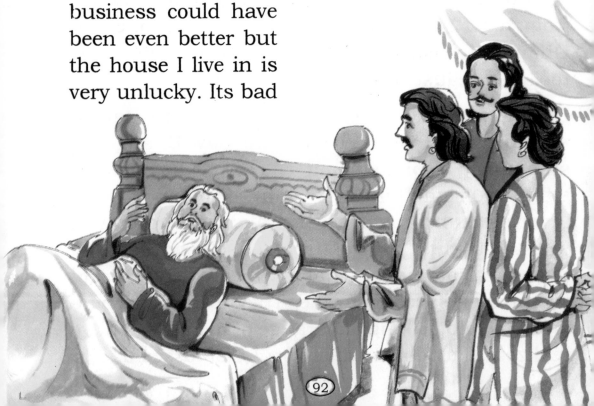

luck has not let me progress and expand my business. I had worked hard to earn the money with which I built this house. I love this house and I want to breathe my last here. People tell me that this house is unlucky because they want me to sell it off at a low price. Then they will buy it for themselves. Now, my sons, you have to prove to them that this house is not unlucky at all. You must stay in this house and earn billions to prove your mettle to the world. That is all I desire my sons!"

Anand and Vinod nodded their heads in agreement but Vivek spoke up. He said, "Father, you have realized your mistakes. It seems in spite of all that,

you are still not going to change at all. You can never be heartless towards your friends and relatives. I think the first thing that you should do is to get yourself away from the business. I think that is very necessary."

Dhangupta accepted the suggestion. Then Vivek continued, "A business must have only one person at the helm of it. Only then will it prosper and expand. So, I request you to appoint any one of us to head your business."

Dhangupta agreed to this, too. He said, "Sons, you are intelligent and hard-workers. I have seen you growing up and I am aware of all the qualities which you lack or possess. One who wants to fulfil my desire must step forward. For the other two, I will give money to start their own business."

At this, Dhangupta's three sons started discussing the matter but they all had the same view. They felt that it was better to expand their father's present

business than to start a new business. That is why they could not reach any decision at that, instantly. They were confused.

Next day, seeing their troubled faces, Dhangupta said, "All right, sons. I'll give a solution to your problem. I will ask the three of you a question. The one who answer my question correctly will become the head of my trade and business."

The merchant's obedient sons agreed to this. Then Dhangupta posed the question to them. He asked,

"Sons, tell me what would you ask for, if God appeared before you and ask you to wish for one boon only?"

To this, Anand replied, "I would ask God to make me the wealthiest man in the world. He must give the whole world's wealth only to me."

Vinod answered the question and said, "I would ask God to provide a comfortable and luxurious life for me. I must have a grand house, wealth, servants and great feasts."

Then it was Vivek's turn to answer. He said, "If God appears before me I'll ask him what a good-hearted person must ask for."

"But it is not clear answer to my question, my son. Tell me clearly what will you ask for?" Dhangupta enquired. Vivek replied, "I will ask God to spread peace and happiness all over the world. I will wish that people all over the world must be healthy and prosperous in life."

Vinod and Anand laughed out aloud on hearing Vivek's reply. But Dhangupta did not laugh at all. He grew thoughtful and later on he declared, "Sons, I have chosen Vivek to head my business.

Anand and Vinod will have to start their own new business."

Anand and Vinod could not understand why their father had chosen Vivek, so they asked for the reason. Dhangupta said, "Sons, all of you are able for that post, so this question was not for testing your abilities. I wanted to test for the selfish streak in you and it is difficult to detect someone's selfishness. That is why I had posed such a question. Your brother Vivek has proved to be more clever and selfish than both of you. That is why I have handed over the business to him."

Then Vetal asked King Vikram, "King Vikram, Dhangupta had learnt the value of selfishness. He had learnt that people wanted to get his house at a cheap price so they had spread a rumour that the house was unlucky. That is why in his old age, he wanted to hand over his business to an able son. But don't you think that he had been foolish to choose

the selfless Vivek for this? Vivek had wished for everyone's prosperity from God just the same as the nature of Dhangupta. Yet Dhangupta had chosen Vivek. Was his decision correct? Tell me now. But remember, I know it well that you know the right answers to my questions. If you will give the right answers to my questions, I will fly back to my banyan tree. But if you will give me the wrong answer even after knowing the correct one, your head will burst into thousand pieces."

King Vikram thought for a while and a few moments later, he replied to the Vetal's questions. He said, "To earn a living, people get engaged in different tasks. That leads to their variety of experiences. Not everyone has the same experience in life. Based on his own life's experiences, one always makes certain type of decisions and has a point of view about life. Based on this, Dhangupta had used his

experiences to learn that ability to prosper business must be accompanied by a streak of selfishness. By listening to his sons' replies, Dhangupta had learnt that each of them was more selfish than the others. But it is also necessary for a selfish person not to display his selfishness for all to know. That's where Anand and Vinod lacked. They told their father about what they wanted from God. A foolish selfish man will lose a lot but an intelligent selfish man will gain from his selfishness. Dhangupta's youngest son, Vivek, was so selfish that even his own father did not know about his selfish nature. He lied about what he would wish from God. He was so selfish that he would not tell anyone, what he would ask from God. Dhangupta had realized this fact and that is why he had chosen Vivek."

Vetal heard King Vikram's reply and, as usual, he flew back to hang on banyan tree.

The Tantrik's Chair

Once again King Vikram went to the banyan tree. He pulled the hanging corpse, slung it on his shoulder and walked on. Then the Vetal said, "King Vikram, I hope that you are not going through all these hardships to gain any kind of favour. Because favours are not received when asked for. People tend to shower favours at unexpected moments. Let me explain this through a story."

A long time ago, there was a forest near Mudrapur. There was an ancient temple in a forest that collapsed. When the king of Mudrapur came to know of this he called his servants and said, "Go to the forest and clear the debris of the temple. After that make arrangements for building materials and labourers. I want a new temple to be constructed at that spot."

So the servants were engaged to clear the debris. As the work was in progress, a labourer discovered a tunnel. When some people went down the tunnel,

they saw that it ended in an underground secret chamber. In the chamber, they found a golden chair. Various strange symbols were drawn on the chair. Soon the king was informed about the chair.

The king grew serious at this news. He said, "I know about that chair. It belongs to the *tantrik* who resided in that temple. When he died, no one knew where his magical chair had gone. People wondered if he had destroyed it or hidden it somewhere. So, now we have found the magical chair. It has certain powers. A person must fast for a day, perform some *tantrik* rituals and only then he can sit on that chair. Then whoever he wishes to be destroyed or harmed, that person will surely suffer.

The king said, "Guards, go and get the chair. Keep it in the royal courtyard for public exhibition."

So, the chair was shifted from the ruins to the palace, where it was placed in the courtyard. Guards stood near it for its security. Thousands of people from all over the kingdom came to have a glimpse of that chair. Many people fell down unconscious because they saw the ghost of the *tantrik* sitting on the chair. Once a young *tantrik* somehow broke through the queue and sat in the chair. The guards got him out of the chair and threw him out of the palace grounds.

Hearing of all this chaos, the king ordered the chair to be shifted to a chamber inside the palace. Public was not allowed to see it anymore. Nearly half a dozen men were ordered to guard the chair. No one could enter the chamber at all.

A learned scholarly priest had earned the king's favour. He used to visit the king everyday and the king consulted him for many matters. One morning, the priest's friend named Puneet came to visit him. He had come to meet the priest after nearly twenty years so the priest was happy to meet his old friend. Puneet said, "Friend, I have come all the way from the village to see the *tantrik's* magical chair. Now it is no longer kept for public view. You are very close to the king. I think you can

 make him grant the permission for me to see the chair."

Hearing this, the priest grew serious. He said, "No, I am not close to the king. He will never

allow anyone to see the chair."

Puneet did not say anything. He went back to the guest-house he was living in. Next day Puneet met the priest and said, "My friend, I met many people in the palace yesterday. I told everyone that I am your friend. They all told me that the king will listen to your request and with your help let me get a glimpse of the chair."

But the priest shook his head and said, "Puneet, the king won't agree to let anyone see the magical chair. Now will you leave me alone, please. I am worried about my cousin at present. He is ill because an evil spirit has possessed him."

Puneet did not react at all. He simply went back to the guest-house. Next morning, Puneet met the priest once again. He said, "My friend, I met the chief-guard near the chamber today. He is on the duty to guard the chair. He said that he would open the chamber doors for me to see the chair. But I need someone close to the king to accompany me inside the palace. Will you help me out tomorrow ?"

The priest looked very worried. He said, "My friend, why are you taking such pains to see that chair ? Here I have more important tasks at hand. I am suffering with unusual physical pains. Somebody is using black magic to harm me. Don't tell this to anyone. You are my friend so I am revealing this to you."

Poor Puneet went away disappointed. The priest rushed to the king and said, "Your Majesty, the chief-guard who is on the duty for guarding the magical chair is not to be trusted. I have news that he allow their friends into the chamber to see the magical chair."

The king heard this and immediately ordered that the chief-guard be changed from the chamber duty. Next day, when Puneet gained permission to enter the palace through a courtier's word, the chief-guard said, "Sir, I am no longer on duty at the chamber door, so it's no use going into the palace."

Puneet felt down but decided to keep trying. He went to meet a minister and said, "Ah ! At last one of my two wishes have come true. I have meet you after much waiting."

The minister was impressed by such flattery, so he said, "I am impressed. What is your second wish ?"

"To get a small glimpse of the *tantrik's* magic chair. I heard that it is in a guarded chamber inside the royal palace." Puneet expressed his second wish.

"Oh ! Is that all ! Come to the palace and meet me at the western gate at ten o'clock in the morning. I will take you to the chamber with me."

Puneet's heart was filled with joy at this news. He ran and told about this to his friend. But the priest grew serious and thoughtful. That evening, the priest happened to meet the minister at a social function. By chance, the minister mentioned about his meeting with Puneet and how he was going to help him to see the chair. The priest merely said, "Yes, go on, show the chair to him. But you must be ready for the consequences !"

The minister realized what the priest was trying to say. At night he thought of refusing Puneet.

Next day, Puneet met the minister at the appointed place and time but the minister said, "I apologize to you. I could not get the king's approval for the visit."

When Puneet was about to go, one of the minister's companion requested him to let Puneet see the chair for he had wasted much of his time for this. But the minister whispered to his companion, "The priest told me about the risk involved. I do not want to get into any trouble for a mere villager !"

As luck would have it, Puneet heard these words. He was shocked to learn that his friend had been frustrating all his efforts of seeing the *tantrik's* chair. He felt very hurt. He went to the guest-house and packed his belongings. He was soon ready to go back to the village. He went to the priest's house to bid good-bye. He said, "Good-bye, old friend. I am leaving for the village now."

The priest embraced him and said, "I am sorry, my friend. All my influences could not help you to see the magical chair."

"Well ! But your influence was clearly seen in the way all my efforts were failed !" Puneet commented in a bitter tone. With this, Puneet went out of the priest's house.

Just as Puneet reached out of the gates of his house, the priest stopped him and said, "Puneet, my friend, wait a moment. You cannot go away like this. You must stay with me for a few days. Be my guest. I'll go and try my luck with the king. Maybe he will grant the permission after all. Come and let us have a grand feast together."

Puneet was stunned to see this change in the priest's behaviour. But he felt happy that he would see the chair and would not lose a dear friend. Then the friends embraced and sat to eat a tasty feast with a variety of dishes. They enjoyed the feast and talked about old times.

Next morning, the priest obtained the king's permission. He went with Puneet to see the *tantrik's* magical chair in the guarded chamber. Then Puneet returned to the priest's house. After spending three days with his friend, Puneet left for his village.

Then Vetal asked King Vikram, "O king ! Now it is the time to tell me some facts. Don't you think the priest acted strangely ? After all the efforts made by Puneet to see the chair, the priest did his best to let him not see the chair and then suddenly he changed his behaviour and led his friend to the chamber himself. Now you tell me what all this meant ? But remember, I know it well that you know the right answers to my questions. If you will give the right answers to my questions, I will fly back to my banyan tree. But if you will give me wrong answer even after knowing the correct one, your head will burst into thousand pieces."

A few thoughtful moments later, King Vikram replied, "The priest was scared of Puneet's unknown intentions. Why would a long lost friend contact the priest and come from a far away village just to see a chair ? The priest thought maybe Puneet was some

tantrik and wanted to get the chair. He did not want to aid Puneet to harm someone through the chair's harmful magical powers. So he acted in ways that the guard and the minister would not lead Puneet to the chamber. So he cautioned the king about the guard and hinted his views for the minister. To confirm if Puneet had some *tantrik* powers or not, the priest told a false tale about his cousin's illness due to an evil

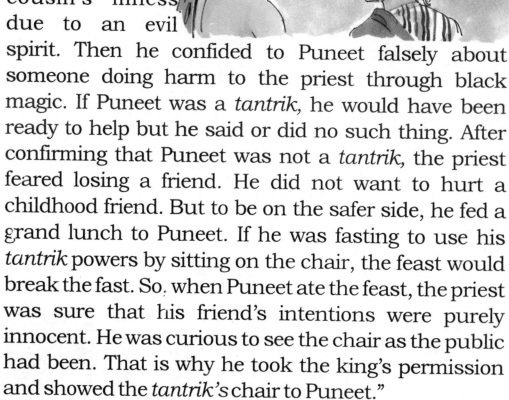

spirit. Then he confided to Puneet falsely about someone doing harm to the priest through black magic. If Puneet was a *tantrik*, he would have been ready to help but he said or did no such thing. After confirming that Puneet was not a *tantrik*, the priest feared losing a friend. He did not want to hurt a childhood friend. But to be on the safer side, he fed a grand lunch to Puneet. If he was fasting to use his *tantrik* powers by sitting on the chair, the feast would break the fast. So, when Puneet ate the feast, the priest was sure that his friend's intentions were purely innocent. He was curious to see the chair as the public had been. That is why he took the king's permission and showed the *tantrik's* chair to Puneet."

At this reply, the Vetal said, "Yes, that's indeed a well thought answer. But now you have broken your promise, I am leaving you."

And Vetal flew back to the branch of the banyan tree.

The Learned Fool

King Vikram went to the banyan tree and climbed up to get the corpse once again. He pulled up the corpse, slung it on his shoulder and walked on towards the cremation ground where the monk was waiting for him. On the way, Vetal said, "King Vikram, I am very impressed by you because so many times I have left you but you never give up hope. With renewed spirit you come to take me again and again. I wonder who is encouraging you to act this way- the learned one inside you or the fool in you. Because every person has these traits hidden in him or her. Many a times, the fool inside a man takes over the learned nature. I suspect its the same with you, too, because being a king you have left your palace to roam in the dark cremation ground. Let me tell you about a foolish young man's story."

A long time ago, the kingdom of Chakravak was ruled by King Shashidhar. His only daughter named

Shampalata was very beautiful. Her beauty could just not be described in words. According to the customs of Chakravak no maiden or woman was allowed to see a man who was not her father or brother. Shampalata had never gone out of the palace, so no one knew how beautiful she was or how she looked.

One day Shampalata requested her father that she wanted a statue made of herself. King Shashidhar wanted to fulfil his dear daughter's wish. So King Shashidhar had it announced that the person who would make the sculpture of his beautiful daughter would be given the title of the royal sculptor. Many sculptors heard the announcement. They knew it very well that Princess Shampalata would not pose for the statue. They would have to use their imagination to sculpt a beautiful maiden's statue which must resemble the princess as much as possible. Many skilled sculptors gathered in the capital. They all worked to sculpt beautiful statues of breath-taking girl. They sent their statues to the palace but none of the statue's beauty came anywhere near that of Shampalata's true beauty.

A young sculptor named Viraj Sharma was returning to Chakravak from Vajrakut. He had gone to Vajrakut for training as a sculptor. Now he had come back to his parents in Chakravak. He also heard the royal announcement. His father Pradeep Sharma was a great sculptor. He was now old and had stopped sculpting. When Viraj Sharma reached home, he asked his father how anyone could make a girl's statue without seeing her.

Pradeep Sharma laughed and said, "Son, your curiosity is obvious. Many sculptors are worried by the condition set by the king. This task seems impossible but *yoga* and *tantrik* power possessors can make this task easy. Through *yoga* meditation and complete concentration, one can imagine a certain face before one's eyes. The sculptors of ancient times used to gain this sight through *yoga*. That is why they were able to make beautiful sculpts of gods and goddesses on temple and cave walls. This feat can be achieved through *tantra* and chants, too, but this knowledge is possessed by the *yakshas* only who in turn help the artists. To the north of our country lies Aranya. In that country on every *amavasya* (No moon night) the *yakshas* gather

together. They are most learned in *tantra* and *mantra*. With their help, you can attain success for sure. The night after tomorrow is *amavasya*."

To this Viraj Sharma said, "But how can I take help from their powers ? I want to make the statue of the princess and become the royal sculptor."

"Don't waste time. Be courageous and try your best. I will be happy if you achieve this aim. Many people have had the blessings of *yakshas* and had their impossible wishes coming true. You must go and try your luck at it !" Pradeep Sharma advised his son.

With such encouraging words and his father's blessings, Viraj Sharma left for Aranya next morning. He rode his horse and reached Aranya on the evening of the *amavasya* night. He was feeling very tired, so he took out some food, ate it and then he slept off under a shady tree.

He woke up a few hours later when he heard someone's voice. He opened his eyes and saw two gorgeous young girls. Their tinkling laughter was resounding all around. They were adorned in gold ornaments from head to toe. Seeing them, Viraj

Sharma realized that they were certainly *yaksha-kanyas*. He was so scared that he became speechless. The next moment one of them approached him and said, "Young man, what brings you here on this dark moonless night?"

Viraj Sharma bowed to them respectfully and told them the purpose of his visit. Then one of the *yaksha-kanya* said, "It is indeed a hard task to make someone's statue without seeing him or her. But both of us will make it possible for you. My name is Chapala and she is called Chanchala. We want to have our statues made to adorn the valley here. If you promise to make our statues then we will be willing to help you."

Viraj Sharma agreed to the condition. The next moment, Chapala snapped her finger and chanted a verse. Then she touched Chanchala who turned into a breath-takingly attractive girl. Viraj Sharma had never seen such a beautiful girl before.

"Where is Chanchala?" Viraj Sharma asked in surprise.

"She is right here. She has changed into Princess Shampalata. Now she will pose as the

model for Princess Shampalata's statue. We will empower your tools with ten hundred times their usual speed." Saying so, Chapala provided him white marble, "You must start sculpting now."

So Viraj Sharma started sculpting with the help of his fast tools. He completed Princess Shampalata's statue in two days time. The statue had been sculpted with great skill indeed.

Then Viraj Sharma said, "As you have helped me, I am very thankful to you. Do me another favour. Please make some arrangement to carry this statue to my house. I cannot carry it all the way to my country. I promise to return on next *amavasya* to sculpt your statues."

Chapala snapped her fingers and Viraj Sharma found himself and the statue in the courtyard of his house in Chakravak. He thanked the *yaksha-kanyas* in his heart. Then he rushed into the house and met his father. He told him all that had happened and showed him his work, too.

Next day Viraj Sharma sent a message to King Shashidhar that the statue of Princess Shampalata was ready. Arrangements were made to carry the statue to the palace. Then the king and his family saw the statue in their private chamber. They were stunned to see the beauty and skill reflected in the work. The king felt that he was not seeing a statue but was seeing his daughter Shampalata standing before him. Princess Shampalata was overjoyed to see the statue. She was very impressed with Viraj Sharma. She exclaimed, "Oh ! I think I am seeing my reflection in the mirror. This does not appear to be the work of a human being. I think some magical powers have sculpted it."

Then King Shashidhar kept his words. On an auspicious day, he said that Viraj Sharma would be declared royal sculptor of Chakravak. He called Viraj Sharma and said, "I am impressed by your work. Your statue is matchless, I don't think there is a greater sculptor than you in this whole world. My brother's daughter Manjula has come here from Shamantak Nagar to see the sculpture. She saw the statue and praised your skill a lot. She has the keen desire that you should make a similarly beautiful statue of her, too. Two days after making her

statue I'll honour you with the title of the royal sculptor and you will be given gifts and rewards for your skilful art."

Instead of being happy and excited at the king's words, Viraj Sharma became dull and discouraged. His face lost the glow of pride. Then he took his leave from King Shashidhar.

Viraj Sharma went home and said to his father, "Father, tomorrow morning we must leave for my *guru's ashram* in Vajrakut. It is outside our country's border and the king who rules there is more learned and able than King Shashidhar."

So, without any more discussion, Viraj Sharma's family left Chakravak and went off to settle down in Vajrakut.

Then Vetal addressed King Vikram, "King Vikram, Viraj Sharma was a great and skilled sculptor. He was an intelligent young man but there was a foolish streak in his nature. He went under the influence of the fool in him and lost the chance to earn fame, name and wealth. There was once a time when he wished with all his heart to become the royal sculptor and he undertook a laborious journey to fulfil his desire. And then just when he was to be honoured as the royal sculptor, his jest for life, fame, name and wealth vanished into thin air. Without thinking he let go off the golden opportunity he was about to receive. Just as he had made the statue of Princess Shampalata with *yaksha-kanya's* help, he could have done the same to create Manjula's statue. Then he would easily have enjoyed a luxurious and famous life. But he left all this and went away to Vajrakut. Don't you think it was utterly foolish to act this way ? I think he turned out to be a learned fool. Tell me what you think about him. But remember, I know it well that you know the right answers to my questions. If you will give the right answers to my questions, I will fly back to my banyan tree. But if you will give me the wrong answer even after knowing the correct one, your head will burst into thousand pieces."

A few moments later, King Vikram spoke up, "Many strange rites and rules are known in this world. The same way it was the custom of King Shashidhar's family that no one could see the face of the princess yet one must make her statue. This was a senseless and illogical condition for any sculptor. Still Viraj Sharma took his father's advice to take help of the *yaksha-kanyas* to fulfil this

almost impossible condition. When Viraj Sharma fulfilled the condition, King Shashidhar did not even try to find out how he had sculpted the princess without having seen her. This reflected the king's foolishness. Viraj Sharma had not taken the position of the royal sculptor yet he was given the task of making Manjula's statue. Viraj Sharma wondered how many more girls he would need to sculpt without seeing them. It would be impossible to take the *yaksha-kanyas'* help again and again. So, after thinking over, he decided that it was better to work for a art-loving king of Vajrakut than for a foolish king of Chakravak. He knew it was best for him and for his father to leave Chakravak. That is why Viraj Sharma's decision to leave the chance of becoming royal sculptor of Chakravak was a very intelligent one."

Vetal heard King Vikram's answer and said, "King Vikram, your answer has confirmed what I had heard about you. You are a clear headed and able ruler. But you have spoken and broken your promise, so I am leaving you, farewell."

With these words, Vetal flew back to his home tree.

Precious Pink Pearl

Firmly determined King Vikram went back to the banyan tree. He climbed the tree once again to get the corpse. He pulled the corpse, slung it on his shoulder, climbed down the tree and then he walked on towards the monk. To make his task easy, Vetal spoke up, "King Vikram, as I have realized, you are really a courageous and a man of firm determination. But are you sure that you are wise also ? I ask you this because you are trying to get me again and again without thinking of the result of your actions. I'll tell you a story of a man who acted in such a way."

King Chitrasen was a great and wise king. He reigned over Virpuri. He had a small private museum in his palace, where he preserved many rare and unique objects. He had collected them from various places in the world. The most

strange object of his hoarding was a pink pearl. Its colour, texture and shine was beyond compare.

When King Chitrasen grew old, he decided to divide all his royal wealth, property and rare objects amongst his three sons. So he made three equal shares of the same. But he felt it hard to give away the precious pink pearl. It was his most loved

object. He wanted to give it to the son who would know its true worth.

The three princes of King Chitrasen were named, Chatursen, Mitrasen and Virsen. The king called all the three of them and said, "Sons, I have something important to tell you. I have given you equal shares from my wealth and property. But I have a precious pink pearl. For it is a single piece so I have decided to give it to the one who, I think, is intelligent, humble and noble at heart. For this, I have set a test for you. All of you must go and live as simple citizen, for a year. You must come back and tell me about one noble deed that you did during that year. The one I think to be the noblest of the three, will get this precious pink pearl."

So next day, the three brothers went away to different places. Time flew by and soon a year was past. The three brothers returned to the royal palace. King Chitrasen asked Chatursen, "Son, tell me about your noblest act in the last year."

To this Prince Chatursen said, "Father, I went to the neighbouring kingdom. There, in the city, I worked as an accountant in a rich jeweller's shop. One day, he gave me a big bag full of diamonds and other gems. When he gave it to me, he had not counted them. Then he asked me to take the bag to another merchant in the nearby town. On the way, I could have stolen some of the diamonds or gems and my master would not have come to know about it. But I kept my sense of integrity and honesty. I did not steal any of the diamonds or gems. When

the other merchant received the full bag, he praised me. He wrote a letter to my master certifying my honesty."

Then King Chitrasen asked second son,

"Dear Prince Mitrasen, is there anything that reflects your noble attitude ?"

To this Prince Mitrasen replied, "Father, when I left the palace, I went towards our neighbouring country in the north. I was riding my horse. On the way, I felt thirsty and saw that my horse was also tired. So I stopped by a river near our country's border. I refreshed myself after washing my face and drank some river-water. My horse also drank the water. I tied him to a shady tree. Then I lay their and dozed off because I, too, was very tired. A few minutes later, I heard someone shouting. I woke up and looked around. I saw a child was flowing away in the swift-moving river-water. His desperate mother was shouting for help. She was standing on the bank because she could not swim. Without thinking of the consequences I ran and jumped into the river. After a few minutes' struggle, I finally reached the child and dragged him to the river-bank. His mother thanked me profusely."

Prince Mitrasen completed his tale with pride. Then King Chitrasen turned to his youngest son and asked, "Prince Virsen, what noble act did you do in the year gone by ?"

Prince Virsen narrated his tale of nobility. He said, "I spent the whole year visiting many countries but got no chance to do any noble act at all. I was feeling very dejected as I was coming back to the kingdom. I stopped and spent the night sleeping under a tree. At dawn I woke up and saw a man sleeping at the edge of a cliff. On the other side was a deep gorge. If he would roll over once in his sleep, he would straight away fall into the deep gorge. It seemed that he had gone and slept there in the dark night and had not seen what a dangerous spot he had chosen. So I rushed up the cliff. Just as I was about to wake up the man, I saw his face. He was my enemy. We both hated each other and he had tried to kill me many a times. I knew even if I saved his life now, he would not thank me. But I could not help myself. I woke him up and showed him the deep gorge he might have fallen into. As expected, he merely glared at me in hatred and, without a word of thanks, he walked away. But I felt relieved that I had saved someone's life even if it was my enemy's."

King Chitrasen heard Virsen's tale.

Then he retired to his bed-chamber to think over his sons' tales. In the evening, he summoned his sons again and said, "My sons, after hearing your stories, I have decided to hand over my precious pink pearl to the youngest of your brothers. Prince Virsen, my son, please take this pearl and keep it as carefully as I have."

Vetal completed the story and then asked King

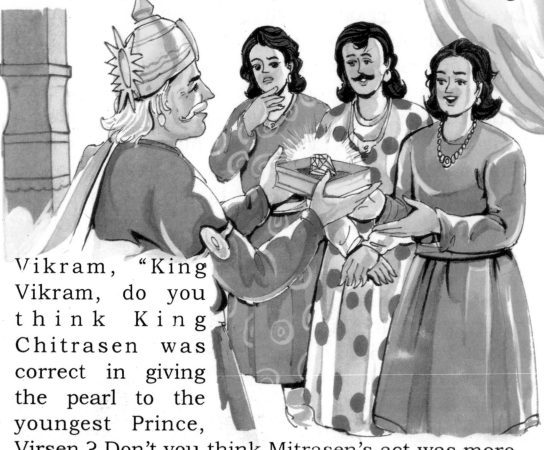

Vikram, "King Vikram, do you think King Chitrasen was correct in giving the pearl to the youngest Prince, Virsen ? Don't you think Mitrasen's act was more heroic as he jumped into a river to save a child ? What do you think about Chatursen ? Was he not a symbol of honesty and integrity when he did not steal even any of the precious diamonds and gems entrusted to him ? I think King Chatursen was blinded by the love for his youngest son, Prince

Virsen. He had only tried to waken up a stupid man who had slept at the edge of a cliff. Was it more noble than the other brothers' acts ? Think about it carefully and tell me now. But remember, I know it well that you know the right answers to my questions. If you give the right answers to my questions, I will fly back to my banyan tree. But if you give me the wrong answer even after knowing the correct one, your head will surely burst into thousand pieces."

Without any waste of time, King Vikram spoke up. He said, "King Chatursen's choice displayed his wisdom very clearly. His choice of Prince Virsen was the best indeed. Prince Chatursen's act was one that displayed honesty but it was not a noble act. If he had stolen the diamonds and gems, then he would have been called a thief. He did not steal because he did not want to be ashamed when everyone called him a thief. So, in a way, he had acted this

way for his own benefit. On the other hand, Prince Mitrasen had saved a drowning child. The act displays his courage and presence of mind. He had received thanks for that act from the child's mother. But it was Prince Virsen who acted in a noble way. When he found out that the man he wanted to save was his enemy, he did not walk away. It was his natural nobleness that led him on to act. He knew that he would not gain much out of this. He acted without any desire or fear of consequences at the hands of his enemy. That is why noble Prince Virsen was rightly gifted with the precious pink pearl."

Vetal commented, "King Vikram, your explanation has indeed satisfied my probing mind. Now I will leave you for you have spoken and broken your promise."

With these words Vetal flew back to his home tree.

Prince Mritunjay's Lesson

When once again King Vikram went back to the banyan tree, he saw the corpse hanging on its usual branch. He climbed up the tree and brought down the corpse. Then he hung it on his shoulder and went on towards the monk.

Again Vetal addressed King Vikram and said, "King Vikram, I see that you are taking pains to help someone else's work. There are many people in this world who do not work to perform even their own duties. Some of them don't even realize their own responsibilities until someone else enlightens them. I will tell you the story of such a person. Now listen to the story carefully."

Once upon a time, the kingdom of Jayapuri was ruled by King Jayadev. Being a kind and wise king, his kingdom had the loyalty of his subjects and the blessings of Gods. Thus, his kingdom was a prosperous one and everyone there lived a

comfortable and content life. He had a son named Prince Mritunjay.

As King Jayadev grew old, he began to be sad and worried. Soon he took to the bed and became very ill. The reason of his illness was the prince who had been pampered. Although the prince was an intelligent, obedient and handsome young man and the king had got the prince trained under great scholars and warriors, yet he used to worry a lot. Because the prince did not have the qualities, duties and responsibilities needed to be a king. He used to love going on hunting trips and would spend time and money on his friends. King Jayadev wondered how he could hand over the reigns of the kingdom in the hands of such a careless young man.

One day, a famed learned hermit named Swami Jitendriya visited Jayapuri. The king welcomed him with warm feelings. He offered him food and a special chamber in the royal palace. Swami Jitendriya observed the lines of worry on King Jayadeva's forehead. He went to the king's chamber and asked him in private as to what was worrying him. King Jayadev told Swami Jitendriya about the irresponsible Prince Mritunjay. To this, Swami Jitendriya said, "King Jayadev, do not worry. I know exactly how to solve your problem. Just send Prince Mritunjay to my chamber early in the morning tomorrow."

The king agreed to this and asked Prince Mritunjay to meet Swami Jitendriya. Next morning, the prince went to meet him. He bowed to the hermit respectfully and said, "Holy sir, my father sent me to you. I am honoured to meet you."

Swami Jitendriya smiled and said, "Son, I know you are a strong and brave young man. I want your help in some work."

"Sir, I would be honoured to be at your service," the prince humbly said.

"I will presently give you an earthen pot. It contains juices of many rare herbs. I have taken great pains to search for the rare herbs and to extract their juices. This is to be used in a grand *yajna* due to be performed in my *ashram* the day after tomorrow. Without this, the rites of the *yajna* will not be complete. This would anger the

Gods and the lives of my disciples and myself will be in grave danger." Swami said.

"What role do I have in all this, holy sir ?" Prince Mritunjay asked.

"Son, some urgent work has come up. So I cannot leave for the *ashram* now. But this pot of juice must reach the *ashram* as soon as possible. Being a brave boy you can carry this pot from the palace, through the dense forest, to my *ashram* situated at the border of Jayapuri in the east across the river. I want you to carry the pot carefully. Not even one drop of this precious juice must fall to the ground. I have called you to take over this task for me."

Prince Mritunjay agreed to this obediently. Swami Jitendriya handed over the pot full of herbal juice to him. He packed some food for Prince Mritunjay and advised him to depart soon. Putting the pot of herbal juice in a tiny trunk, he hung it by a rope around his neck. Then he sat on the horse and rode towards the *ashram*.

As Prince Mritunjay rode on, he had to pass

through a dense forest. He bravely rode through the forest. A few minutes later, a big elephant appeared at the end of the path. He was in a very angry mood. When he saw Prince Mritunjay on horse's back, he rushed towards him with great speed. Immediately, Prince Mritunjay drew out the sword from his waist. He was about to approach the elephant and to strike at him when he stopped suddenly. He was reminded of the trunk around his neck. Any attacking movement of his body would disturb the pot. Prince Mritunjay was afraid that this would surely spill the rare juice. So the alert prince saw a path branching away through a nearby grove of trees. He turned his horse towards that path

and rode away at great speed. In a few moments he was far away from the raging elephant.

By noon it had grown pretty hot. Prince Mritunjay was feeling tired, hungry and thirsty. As luck would have it, he soon saw the river he was to cross. So he decided to stop and rest for a while before crossing the river. He thought that he would place the little trunk by the river bank and freshen up a little. Just when he was about to get off the horse, a thought flashed through his mind. He thought, "What if I kept this trunk on the river bank and some animal would meddle with it ? It may be knocked off and the herbal juice will be spilled. No, I think I must go on. I can rest a while at the *ashram* or on my way back."

So Prince Mritunjay changed his mind and continued his journey. He suppressed his desire to stop and eat the food, packed for him in a bag. Soon he skilfully led his horse across the river through the spot where the water was rather shallow. Once again he found himself in a small forest. Just then he saw a beautiful deer running out from the bushes. The prince loved hunting so he at once took aim with his bow to kill the deer. But once again he remembered the pot he was carrying. Chasing the deer would surely cause the herbal juice to spill. So Prince Mritunjay controlled himself once again.

By evening Prince Mritunjay reached the *ashram* at the end of the forest. There he met

Swami Jitendriya's disciples and handed over the pot to them. All this time he had not spilled even a single drop of the precious juice. Then he heaved a sigh of relief and started the journey to the palace. He did not stop to rest in the night. He rode back through the forest and across the river all through the  night. At dawn, Prince Mritunjay reached back in the royal palace in Jayapuri. Then he went to Swami Jitendriya's chamber. After paying his respects, he stood aside. Swami Jitendriya said, "I am glad you could carry out this task successfully. Thank you, son !"

But Prince Mritunjay spoke in a humble tone, "Holy sir, I should be the one to thank you. You have surely enlightened me. Now I have realized my duties and responsibilities. I will try to make my father happy by being a kind and wise ruler like him. Please bless me that I may succeed."

Swami Jitendriya blessed Prince Mritunjay with a smile. When King Jaydev heard this news, his heart was filled with joy. He embraced Prince Mritunjay and from that day the king never felt ill.

He was always happy and smiling. Soon he gave the royal throne's responsibility to Prince Mritunjay and went to spend the rest of his life in Swami Jitendriya's *ashram*.

Then Vetal asked King Vikram, "King Vikram, what do you think which caused the sudden change in Prince Mritunjay's nature ? Was it King Jayadev's illness that made him change or was it some magical powers of Swami Jitendriya ? Tell me the answers. But remember, I know it well that you have the right answers to my questions. If you will give the right answers to my questions, I will fly back to my banyan tree. But if you give me the wrong answer even after knowing the correct one, your head will surely burst into thousand pieces."

As usual, King Vikram had an explanation to Vetal's queries. So he said, "Swami Jitendriya sent Prince Mritunjay on a journey through the dense forest and across the river. It was not the journey but the pot of herbal juice which made Mritunjay responsible for his acts. If he had fought the elephant, stopped to rest or

killed the deer, he would have spilled the juice. This sense of responsibility and caring guided his actions. He had to control his own personal desires to be able to carry out his responsibility entrusted by the great swami. Ruling over a kingdom with vast territory, enormous wealth and trusting subjects was a similar responsibility but of a greater proportion. Just as he was responsible for the safety of the herbal juice, he would have to care for his peoples' safety. This realization dawned upon Prince Mritunjay during and after the responsible journey. That is what caused the sudden change in his attitude and behaviour."

Vetal once again admired King Vikram. He said, "King Vikram, I admire your ability to look deeply into a situation and analyse it well. Truly, I was expecting such a clever answer from you. But by speaking up now you have not kept your word. So I am going back where I came from."

And Vetal flew away to the banyan tree once again.

An Amazing Tale

As usual King Vikram climbed up the banyan tree again. He pulled the corpse, slung it on his shoulder and started his journey towards the monk waiting for him. In the way, Vetal began his tale. He said, "King Vikram, I will now ask you the greatest question of all. But first you must hear this story."

A long time ago, Dakshinpath was ruled by a Mandalik king named Dharmaraj. He had married a decent girl from Malwa. They had a beautiful daughter named Lavanyavati. King Dharmaraj's relatives were jealous of him and were always working to harm him. Years went by like this. Lavanyavati had now reached marriageable age. The king's cruel relatives staged a coup and overthrew him. To save his own life and that of his wife and daughter, King Dharmaraj left his kingdom at night. They decided to go away to Malwa. Before fleeing they took some precious gems and gold coins along.

They walked on and spent the night in a forest. At the dawn, they continued their journey and soon reached another forest. The royal family was used to

luxuries and comforts. As they walked, their soft feet got cut by stones, pebbles and thorns. Soon they passed through a village of Bhil community. The Bhils were cruel in nature and were dacoits. When they saw the king, they attacked him. The king sent his wife and daughter to hide in the nearby woods immediately. Then he fought valiantly with the Bhils. But they were a large group and soon the king was killed. The Bhils took away the gold coins and the gems he carried. The queen and the princess saw this from behind a grove in the woods. Then they ran off into deeper woods to save their lives. Soon they reached a small stream. They sat on its bank and started crying.

In the woods, King Chandra Singh and his son Prince Singhparakram were busy hunting. They saw the footprints of them in the soft, wet earth near the stream. One pair of footprints was of tiny, delicate feet while the other pair of footprints were of someone with bigger feet. Seeing this, they decided to follow the footprints. The prince said, "Father, I lost my mother a few months ago. You are also lonely now. I think when we find the two women I will marry the one whose feet are tiny for surely she must be younger in age. You must promise me to marry the woman who has the bigger feet. So that you, too, will have a life partner."

King Chandra Singh gave his word. Then the two of them founded the queen and the princess by the stream. When they saw the two horsemen, they stopped crying. They feared that they were also dacoits. But then King Chandra Singh introduced himself and reassured them about their safety. Then the queen and the princess calmed down. The king and the prince brought them to their royal palace in the kingdom.

Surprisingly the Queen had the tiny and delicate feet while the Princess Lavanyavati had the big feet.

So a few weeks later, King Chandra Singh kept the word he had given to Prince Singhparakra. The king married Princess Lavanyavati because, according to the promise, he had to marry the woman with the bigger feet. The queen had the tiny, delicate feet so Prince

Singhparakram had to marry her. Thus, it so happened that Princess Lavanyavati became her own mother's mother-in-law. As years went by, they gave birth to sons and daughters and then they also had grand children.

Then Vetal laughed out aloud and said, "King Vikram, tell me now how the children of the mother and daughter were related to each other ? But remember, I know it well that you know the right answers to my questions. If you will give the right answers to my questions, I will fly back to my banyan tree. But if you will give me wrong the answer even after knowing the correct one, your head will burst into thousand pieces."

King Vikram grew thoughtful at this great question. He did not know what to say so he walked on in silence with the corpse hung on his shoulder. The Vetal who had occupied the corpse thought to himself, "Now, this is a question perhaps King Vikram cannot answer. I think the time has come to teach a lesson to the monk who has made King Vikram go through all this. I will now gift the magical powers to this just and wise king. I will not let the powers go in the hands of an evil monk at all."

Then Vetal spoke aloud to King Vikram. He said, "King Vikram, you passed through this horrifying place all night long so many times. Yet you have not strayed from your determination. For this, you must be richly rewarded. Now I will leave this corpse. You can take the corpse to the monk. But before I leave, I want to tell you something. You must listen to this very carefully and attentively."

Vetal continued, "King Vikram, the monk who has asked you to get the corpse is an evil man. Tonight, he will try to call me back into the corpse after performing certain rites. Then he would want to cut off your head to sacrifice it during the ritual. For this, he will ask you to prostrate yourself before him. Then you must ask him to show that how to prostrate to offer respect. When he bows low to demonstrate, you must quickly chop off the monk's head with your sword. Even the delay of a moment will surely spell disaster. Now go on your way. May you attain success in your endeavour!"

With these words, Vetal left the corpse forever. Then, with the corpse on his shoulder, King Vikram went on his way.

Monk Shantishil's Tale

Soon King Vikram reached the banyan tree under which the monk was waiting for him. The dark amavasya night was silent except for the howling of jackals and hooping of owls. The monk sat under the tree. The ground in front of him had been painted with fresh blood. He had made a *tantrik* sign with the powder of ground bones. There were pots full of blood kept all around. A lamp had been lit with human fat. A fire was burning nearby. But all these objects covered with blood did not deter King Vikram's steps.

King Vikram went near to the monk. The monk's face lit up with joy when he saw King Vikram with the corpse on his shoulder. He stood up with folded hands and said, "King Vikram ! You have obliged me. People speak the truth when they speak of your helpful and kind nature. Learned people say that this is the trait of great rulers."

Then the monk took the corpse off King Vikram's shoulder and bathed it. Then he put some paste on the corpse, garlanded it and kept it in the

centre of the tantrik symbol. Then the monk covered his own body with ash and wore a white cloth which is usually used for covering dead bodies. Then he started meditating.

Using the power of chants, the monk called the Vetal to possess the corpse. Then, after certain rites, he offered some human body parts for the *tantrik* ritual. The monk turned to King Vikram and said, "Your Majesty, you must prostrate yourself at this spot. This would please the Gods and you can ask for any boon you desire."

Hearing this, King Vikram was reminded of Vetal's warning. So he said to the monk, "Holy sir, I cannot do so for I do not know the correct way. Please be kind enough to show me how to prostrate correctly. Then I will follow your example."

As soon as the monk bowed low to show how King Vikram must prostrate, King Vikram drew out his shiny, sharp sword and cut off the monk's head. Then he tore the monk's chest open and offered his heart to Vetal. Then Vetal spoke from the corpse once as before. He said, "King Vikram, the magical powers and spiritual wealth that this monk had intended to attain have now been granted to you. You have had to suffer a lot because of me. Now you may ask for any boon you wish for."

To this, King Vikram replied, "Actually your pleasure has made me happy, too. I do not really need anything. But I think I can request you to make all the tales you told me, famous the world over. They must be heard respectfully everywhere."

Vetal said, "O great King Vikram, your wish will be taken care of. But now I'll tell you what I want. I will use my powers to make these tales blessed. So anyone who hears them will be blessed and will gain knowledge and wisdom regarding various phases of life. One who hears or reads these tales will no longer be a sinner. Wherever these tales will be told, no evil spirits would ever wander there."

After saying this, Vetal left the corpse and using his yogic powers he left to the unknown world.

Having observed all this, Lord Shiva

and the other Gods were impressed by King Vikram. So Lord Shiva appeared before him. King Vikram bowed before him with folded hands. Then Lord Shiva said, "Son, you are blessed for having killed the evil monk. He wanted to gain the position of learned scholars and become a *Chakravarti Samrat* through his evil ways. I have created you to stay on Earth to get it rid of all dacoits, corrupt people and evil doers. Whenever you have had enough of this world, you can wish and willingly come to me anytime. Now you will be known as *Aparajit* that is the one who can never be defeated. Go and spend your life with my blessings."

Then Lord Shiva disappeared. King Vikram rode his horse through the night and after an hour, dawn broke out. So after completing his task, King Vikram went back to his capital. Gradually the people and scholars learnt about all these events and praised King Vikram highly.